Dean Koontz was born into a very poor family and learned early on to escape into fiction – though books were scorned by his parents as a waste of time. He won an *Atlantic Monthly* fiction competition in 1965 at the age of twenty. Since then fourteen of his novels have appeared in the national and international bestseller lists and have sold nearly fifty-five million copies worldwide.

He lives in southern California with his wife Gerda.

Shattered

Dean R Koontz

First published in Great Britain in 1974
by Arthur Barker Limited under the name of K R Dwyer

First published in paperback in 1983
by Star Books,
the paperback division of W H Allen & Co PLC

Reprinted in paperback in 1990
by HEADLINE BOOK PUBLISHING PLC

First HEADLINE FEATURE paperback in 1991

10 9 8 7 6 5 4 3

ISBN 0 7472 3523 6

Printed and bound in Great Britain by
Collins, Glasgow

HEADLINE BOOK PUBLISHING PLC
Headline House
79 Great Titchfield Street
London W1P 7FN

**To Lee Wright
in return for
much kindness,
advice,
and patience**

Author's Note

Shattered was written in 1972, when I was only twenty-seven, and published the following year by Random House. Those were the days of anti-war protests and considerable civil disturbance, when the very fabric of our society was severely tested. The predominant mood was paranoia, and I tried to capture the feeling of the times in this novel.

Shattered was published under a pen name (K.R. Dwyer), which I was using at that time for books that were shorter than the novels I published under my own name. Over the years, the novel was used by book clubs, made into a film by Warner Brothers, and translated into ten other languages – all with the Dwyer by-line attached. Burdened with the usual writer's ego, I viewed the book's successes with mixed feelings, more than a little perturbed that all of the credit should accrue to the nonexistent Dwyer. I am delighted, therefore, that *Shattered* is at last in print with its true father revealed. (However, if you should have any complaints, I would prefer that you direct your mail to Mr Dwyer!)

Dean Koontz
Orange, California
1983

Monday

One

Only four blocks from the furnished apartment in Philadelphia, with more than three thousand miles to drive before they joined Courtney in San Francisco, Colin began one of his games. Colin thrived on his games, not those which required a board and movable pieces but those which were played inside the head – word games, idea games, elaborate fantasies. He was a very garrulous and precocious eleven-year-old with more energy than he was able to use. Slender, shy in the company of strangers, bothered by a moderately severe astigmatism in both eyes that required him to wear heavy eyeglasses at all times, he was not much for sports. He could not exhaust himself in a fast game of football, because none of the athletic boys his own age wanted to play with someone who tripped over his own feet, dropped the ball, and was devastated by even the most delicate tackle. Besides, sports bored him. He was an intelligent kid, an avid reader, and he found his own games more fun than football. Kneeling on the front seat of the big car and looking out the rear window at the home he was leaving forever, he said, 'We're being followed, Alex.'

'Are we now?'

'Yeah. He was parked down the block when we put the suitcases in the trunk. I saw him. Now he's following us.'

Alex Doyle smiled as he wheeled the Thunderbird on to the Lansdowne Avenue. 'Big black limousine, is it?'

Colin shook his head, his thick shoulder-length mop of brown hair flopping vigorously. 'No. It's some kind of van. Like a panel truck.'

Alex looked in the rear-view mirror. 'I don't see him.'

'You lost him when you turned the corner,' Colin said. He pressed his stomach against the backrest, head thrust over the back seat. 'There he is! See him now?'

Nearly a block behind them, a new Chevrolet van turned the corner onto Lansdowne Avenue. At five minutes past six o'clock on a Monday morning, it was the only other moving vehicle in sight.

'I thought it was always a black limousine,' Alex said. 'In the movies, the heroes are always followed by a big black limousine.'

'That's only in the movies,' Colin said, still watching the van, which remained a full block behind them. 'Nobody's that obvious in real life.'

The trees on their right cast long black shadows across half the street and made dizzying, flickering patterns on the windshield. The first sun of May had risen somewhat to the east, still too far down the sky for Alex to see it. Crisp spring sunlight bathed the old two-storey frame houses and made them new and fresh again.

Invigorated by the early-morning air and by the spray of green buds on the trees, almost as excited as Colin was about the journey ahead of them, Alex Doyle thought he had never been happier. He handled the heavy car with ease, enjoying the quiet power at his disposal. They were going to be on the road a long time in terms of both hours and miles; but as imaginative as he was, Colin would provide better company than most adults.

'He's still back there,' Colin said.

'I wonder *why* he's following us.'

Colin shrugged his thin shoulders but did not turn around. 'Could be lots of reasons.'

'Name one.'

'Well . . . He could have heard that we were moving to California. He knows we'll take our valuables with us, see? Family treasures, things like that. So he follows us and runs us into a ditch on some lonely stretch of road and robs us at gunpoint.'

Alex laughed. 'Family treasures? All you have is clothes enough for the trip. Everything else went out on the moving van a week ago, or it went with your sister on the plane. And I assure you that I've brought nothing more valuable than my wristwatch.'

Colin was unperturbed by Doyle's amusement. 'Maybe he's an enemy of yours. Somebody with an old grudge to settle. He wants to get hold of you before you leave town.'

'I don't have any real friends in Philly,' Alex said. 'But I don't have any real enemies, either. And if he wanted to beat me up, why didn't he

5

just catch me when I was putting our bags in the trunk?'

Fluttering laces of sunshine and shadow flipped rapidly over the windshield. Ahead, a stoplight turned green just in time to spare Alex the inconvenience of braking.

After a while Colin said, 'Maybe he's a spy.'

'A spy?' Alex asked.

'A Russian or something.'

'I thought we were friends with the Russians these days,' Alex said, looking at the van in the rear-view mirror and smiling again. 'And even if we aren't friends with the Russians these days – why would a spy be interested in you or me?'

'That's easy,' Colin said. 'He has us mixed up with someone else. He was assigned to tail someone living on our block, and he got confused.'

'I'm not scared of any spy who's that inept,' Alex said. He reached out and fiddled with the air-conditioning controls, brought a gentle, cool breeze into the stuffy car.

'He might not be a spy,' Colin said, his attention captured by the unimposing little van. 'He might be something else.'

'Like what?'

'Let me think about it awhile,' the boy said.

While Colin thought about what the man in the van might be, Alex Doyle watched the street ahead and thought about San Francisco. That hilly city was not just a geographical identity so far as Alex was concerned. To him, it was a synonym for the future and a symbol for everything that a man wanted in life. The new job was there, the innovative advertising agency that recognized and cultivated talented young commercial artists. The new house was there, the three-bedroom Spanish stucco on the edge of Lincoln Park, with its spectacular view of the Golden Gate area and the shaggy palm outside the master-bedroom window. And Courtney was there, of course. If she had not been, the new job and the house would not have meant anything. He and Courtney had met in Philadelphia, had fallen in love there, had been married in the city hall on Market Street, with her brother, Colin, as honorary best man and a woman from the Justice Department steno pool as their required adult witness. Then Colin had been packed off to stay two weeks with Alex's Aunt Pauline in Boston, while the newlyweds flew to San Francisco to honeymoon, to meet Alex's new employers to whom he had spoken only over the telephone, and to find and buy the house in which they would start their life together. It was in San Francisco, more than Philly, that the future took shape and meaning. San Francisco *became* the future. And Courtney became inextricably entwined with that city. In Doyle's mind, she *was* San Francisco, just as San Francisco *was* the future. She was golden and even-tempered, exotic, sensuous, intellectually intriguing, comfortable yet exciting – everything that San Francisco was. And now, as he thought about Courtney, the hilly streets and the crisp blue bay rose clearly on the screen behind his eyes.

'He's still back there,' Colin said, peering through the narrow rear window at the van.

'At least he hasn't tried to run us into a ditch yet,' Alex said.

'He won't do that,' Colin said.

'Oh?'

'He'll just tail us. He's a government man.'

'FBI, is he?'

'I think so,' Colin said, grimly compressing his lips.

'Why would he be after us?'

'He's probably got us mixed up with someone else,' Colin said. 'He was assigned to tail some – radicals. He saw our long hair and got confused. He thinks *we're* the radicals.'

'Well,' Alex said, 'our own spies are just as inefficient as the Russians', aren't they?'

Doyle's smile was too large for his face, a generous curve that was punctuated at each end with a dimple. He held the smile both because he felt so damned fine and because he knew that it was the best thing about his face. In all his thirty years, no one had ever told him that he was handsome. Despite the fact that he was one-quarter Irish, there was too much strong-jawed Italian in him, too much of a Roman nose. Three months after they met, when they began to sleep together, Courtney had said, 'Doyle, you are just not a handsome man. You're *attractive*, certainly, but not handsome. When you say that I look smashing, I want to reciprocate – but I just can't lie to you. But your smile . . . Now *that's* perfect. When you smile, you even look a little bit like Dustin Hoffman.' Already they were too honest with each other for Doyle to be hurt by what she'd said. Indeed, he had been delighted by the comparison: 'Dustin Hoffman? You really think so?' She had studied him a moment, putting her hand under his chin and turning his face this way and that in the weak orange light of the bedside lamp. 'When you smile, you look *exactly* like Hoffman – when he's trying to look ugly, that is.' He had gaped at her. 'When he's trying to look *ugly*, for Christ's sake?' She grimaced. 'I meant . . . Well, Hoffman can't really look ugly, even when he tries. When you smile, then, you look like Hoffman but not as handsome . . .' He watched her trying to extricate herself from the embarrassing hole she'd dug, and he had begun to laugh. His laughter had infected her. Soon they were giggling like idiots, expanding on the joke and making it funnier, laughing until they were sick and then settling down and then making love with a paradoxically fierce affection. Ever since that night Doyle tried to remember to smile a lot.

On the right-hand side of the street a sign announced the entrance to the Schuylkill Expressway. 'Give your FBI man a break,' Alex told the boy. 'Let him tail us in peace for a while. The expressway's coming up, so you better turn around and buckle your seatbelt.'

'Just a minute,' Colin said.

'No,' Alex said. 'Get your seatbelt on, or I'll also make you use the shoulder strap.' Colin despised being bound up by both belts.

'*Half* a minute,' the boy said, straining even harder against the back of the seat as Alex drove the car on to the approach ramp leading up to the superhighway.

'Colin—'

9

The boy turned around and bounced down on to the seat. 'I just wanted to see if he followed us on to the expressway. He did.'

'Well, of course he did,' Alex said. 'An FBI man wouldn't be restricted to the city limits. He could follow us anywhere.'

'Clear across the country?' the boy asked.

'Sure. Why not?'

Colin laid his head back against the seat and laughed. 'That'd be funny. What would he do if he followed us clear across country and found out we weren't the radicals he was after?'

At the top of the ramp, Alex looked southeast at the two empty lanes of blacktop. He eased his foot down on the accelerator, and they started west. 'You going to put your seatbelt on?'

'Oh, sure,' Colin said, fumbling for the half of the buckle that was rolled up in the trough beside the passenger's door. 'I forgot.' He had not forgotten, of course. Colin never forgot anything. He just didn't like to wear the belt.

Briefly taking his eyes from the empty highway ahead of them, Alex glanced sideways at the boy and saw him struggling with the two halves of the seatbelt. Colin grimaced, cursed the apparatus, making problems with it so Doyle would know just what he thought of being tied down like a prisoner.

'You might as well grin and bear it,' Alex said, grinning himself as he looked ahead at the highway again. 'You're going to wear that belt the whole way to California, whether you like it or not.'

'I won't like it,' Colin assured him. The seatbelt in place, he smoothed the wrinkles out of his King

Kong T-shirt until the silk-screened photograph of the gigantic, raging gorilla was neatly centred on his frail chest. He pushed his thick hair out of his eyes and straightened the heavy wire-framed glasses which his button nose was hard-pressed to hold in place. 'Thirty-one hundred miles,' he said, watching the grey roadway roll under and behind them. The Thunderbird's power seat elevated high enough to give him a good view. 'How long will it take to drive that far?'

'We won't be lolling around,' Alex said. 'We ought to get into San Francisco Saturday morning.'

'Five days,' Colin said. 'Hardly more than six hundred miles day.' He sounded disappointed by the pace.

'If you could spell me at the wheel,' Alex said, 'we'd do better. But I wouldn't want to handle much more than six hundred a day all by myself.'

'So why didn't Courtney drive out with us?' Colin asked.

'She's getting the house ready. She met the movers there, and she's arranging for drapes and carpeting – all that stuff.'

'Did you know that when I flew up to Boston to stay with Pauline while you two were on your honeymoon – that was my first plane ride?'

'I know,' Alex said. Colin had talked about it for two solid days after he came back.

'I really liked that plane ride.'

'I know.'

Colin frowned. 'Why couldn't we sell this car and fly out to California with Courtney?'

'You know the answer to that,' Alex said. 'The

car's only a year old. A new car depreciates the most in its first year. If you want to get money out of it, you keep it for three or four years.'

'You could afford the loss,' Colin said, beginning to beat a quiet but insistent rhythm on his dungareed knees. 'I heard you and Courtney talking. You'll be making a *fortune* in San Francisco.'

Alex held one palm out to dry it in the hushed breath of the air-conditioning vent on the dashboard. 'Thirty-five thousand dollars a year is not a fortune.'

'I only get a three-dollar allowance,' the boy said.

'True enough,' Alex said. 'But I've got nineteen years of experience and training on you.'

The tyres hummed pleasantly on the pavement.

A huge truck hurtled by on the other side of the road, going in toward the city. It was the first traffic, besides the van, that they had seen.

'Thirty-one hundred miles,' Colin said. 'That's just about one-eighth of the way around the world.'

Alex had to think a minute. 'That's right.'

'If we kept driving and didn't stop in California, we'd need about forty days to circumnavigate the earth,' Colin said, holding his hands around an imaginary globe at which he was staring intently.

Alex remembered when the boy had first learned the word 'circumnavigate' and had been fascinated with the sound and concept of it. For weeks he did not walk around the room or the block — he 'circumnavigated' everything. 'Well, we'd probably need more than forty days,' Alex said. 'I don't know what kind of driving time I can make on the Pacific Ocean.'

Colin thought that was funny. 'I meant we could do it if there was a bridge,' he said.

Alex looked at the speedometer and saw that they were only making a moderate fifty miles an hour, twenty less than he had intended to maintain on this first leg of the journey. Colin was good company. Indeed, he was too good. If he kept distracting Alex, they'd need a month to get across the damn country.

'Forty days,' Colin mused. 'That's half as long as they needed when Jules Verne wrote about it.'

Though he knew that Colin had been skipped ahead one grade in school and that his reading ability was still a couple of years in advance of that of his classmates, Alex was always surprised at the extent of the kid's knowledge. 'You've read *Around the World in Eighty Days*, have you?'

'Sure,' Colin said. 'A long time ago.' He held his hands out in front of another vent and dried them as he had seen Doyle do.

Though it was a small thing, that gesture made an impression on Doyle. He, too, had been a skinny, nervous kid whose palms were always damp. Like Colin, he had been shy with strangers, not much good at sports, an outcast among his contemporaries. In college he had begun a rigorous weight-lifting programme, determined to develop himself into another Charles Atlas. By the time his chest filled out and his biceps hardened, he grew bored with weight-lifting and quit bothering about it. At five-ten and a hundred-sixty pounds, he was no Charles Atlas. But he was slim and hard, and he was no longer the skinny kid either. Still, he was awkward with people whom he had just met – and his palms were often damp with nervous perspiration. Deep inside, he had not forgotten what it was like to be constantly self-conscious and never self-confident enough. Watching Colin dry his slender hands, Alex understood why he had taken an immediate liking to the boy and why they had seemed comfortable with each other from the day they met eighteen months ago. Nineteen years separated them. But little else.

'He still back there?' Colin asked, breaking into Alex's thoughts.

'Who?'

'The van.'

Alex checked the mirror. 'He's there. FBI doesn't give up easily.'

'Can I look?'

'You keep your belt on.'

'This is going to be a bad trip,' Colin said morosely.

'It will be if you don't accept the rules at the start,' Alex agreed.

Traffic picked up on the other side of the expressway as the early-bird commuters began their day and as an occasional truck whistled by on the last lap of a long cargo haul. On the westbound lanes, their own car and the van were the only things in sight.

The sun was behind the Thunderbird, where it could not bother them. Ahead, the sky was marred by only two white clouds. The hills, on both sides, were green.

When they got on the Pennsylvania turnpike at Valley Forge and went west toward Harrisburg, Colin said, 'What about our tail?'

'Still there. Some poor FBI agent tracking the wrong prey.'

'He'll probably lose his job,' Colin said. 'That'll make an opening for me.'

'You want to be an FBI agent?'

'I've thought about it,' Colin admitted.

Alex pulled the Thunderbird into the left lane, passed a car pulling a horse trailer. Two little girls about Colin's age were in the back seat of the car. They pressed against the side window and waved at Colin, who blushed and looked sternly ahead.

'It wouldn't be dull in the FBI,' Colin said.

'Oh, I don't know about that. It might be pretty boring when you have to follow a crook for weeks before he does something exciting.'

'Well, it can't be any more boring than sitting under a seatbelt all the way to California,' Colin said.

God, Alex thought, I walked into that one. He took the car into the right lane again, set the automatic accelerator for an even seventy miles per hour so that if Colin got too interesting they would still make decent time. 'When that guy following us gets us on a lonely stretch of road and runs us into a ditch, you'll thank me for making you wear your belt. It'll save your life.'

Colin turned and looked at him, his big brown eyes made even larger by the eyeglasses. 'I guess you aren't going to give in.'

'You guessed right.'

Colin sighed. 'You're more or less my father now. Aren't you?'

'I'm your sister's husband. But . . . Since your sister has custody of you, I guess you could say I have a father's right to make rules you'll live by.'

Colin shook his head, brushed his long hair out of his eyes. 'I don't know. Maybe it was better being an orphan.'

'Oh, you think so, do you?' Doyle asked, full of mock anger.

'If you hadn't come along, I wouldn't have gotten a plane ride to Boston,' Colin admitted. 'I wouldn't get to go to California either. But . . . I don't know.'

'You're too much,' Doyle said, ruffling the boy's hair with one hand.

Sighing loudly, as if he needed the patience of Job in order to get along with Doyle, the boy smoothed his mussed hair with a comb he kept in his hip pocket. He put the comb away, straightened his King Kong T-shirt. 'Well, I'll have to think about it. I'm just not sure yet.'

The engine was silent. The tyres made almost no noise on the well-surfaced roadbed.

Five minutes slipped by without awkwardness; they were comfortable enough with each other to endure silence. However, Colin grew restless and began to tap wildly elaborate rhythms on his bony knees.

'You want to find something on the radio?' Alex asked.

'I'll have to unbuckle my seatbelt.'

'OK. But just for a minute or two.'

The boy relished the slithering retreat of the cloth belt. In an instant he was on his knees on the seat, turned and looking out the rear window. 'He's still behind us!'

'Hey!' Alex said. 'You're supposed to be finding a radio station.'

Colin turned and sat down. 'Well, you'd have thought I was slipping if I didn't *try*.' His grin was irresistible.

'Get some music on that thing,' Alex said.

Colin fiddled with the AM-FM radio until he located a rock-and-roll show. He set the volume, then suddenly popped up on his knees and looked out the rear window. 'Staying right on our tail,' he said. Then he dropped into his seat and grabbed for his belt.

'You're a real troublemaker, aren't you?' Alex asked.

'Don't worry about me,' the boy said. 'We have to worry about that guy following us.'

At eight-fifteen they stopped at a Howard Johnson's restaurant outside of Harrisburg. The moment Alex slotted the car into a parking space in front of the orange-roofed building, Colin was looking for the van. 'He's here. Like I expected.'

Alex looked out his side window and saw the van pass the front of the restaurant, heading for the service station at the other end. On the side of the white Chevrolet, brilliant blue and green letters read: AUTOMOVER. ONE-WAY MOVE-IT-YOURSELF CONVENIENCE! Then the van was out of sight.

'Come on,' Alex said. 'Let's get some breakfast.'

'Yeah,' Colin said. 'I wonder if he'll have the nerve to walk in after us?'

'He's just here to get gas. By the time we come out, he'll be fifty miles down the turnpike.'

When they came outside again nearly an hour later, the parking spaces in front of the restaurant were all occupied. A new Cadillac, two ageless Volkswagens, a gleaming red Triumph sports car, a battered and muddy old Buick, their own black Thunderbird, and a dozen other vehicles nosed into the kerb like several species of animals sharing a trough. The rented van was nowhere in sight.

'He must have phoned his superiors while we were eating – and discovered he was following the wrong people,' Alex said.

Colin frowned. He jammed his hands into his dungaree pockets, looked up and down the row of cars as if he thought the Chevrolet were really there in some clever new disguise. Now he would have to make up a whole new game.

Which was just as well, as far as Doyle was concerned. It was not likely that even Colin could devise *two* games with built-in excuses for his popping out of his seatbelt every fifteen minutes.

They walked slowly back to the car, Doyle savouring the crisp morning air, Colin squinting at the parking lot and hoping for a glimpse of the van.

Just as they got to the car, the boy said, 'I'll bet he's parked around the side of the restaurant.' Before Doyle could forbid him, Colin jumped back onto the sidewalk and ran around the corner of the building, his tennis shoes slapping loudly on the concrete.

Alex got in the car, started it, and set the air conditioning a notch higher to blow out the stale air that had accumulated while they were having breakfast.

By the time he had belted himself in, Colin was back. The boy opened the passenger's door and climbed inside. He was downcast. 'Not back there either.' He shut and locked the door, slumped down, thin arms folded over his chest.

'Seatbelt.' Alex put the car in gear and reversed out of the parking lot.

Grumbling, Colin put on the belt.

They pulled across the macadam to the service station and stopped by the pumps to have the tank topped off.

The man who hurried out to wait on them was in his forties, a beefy farmer-type with a flushed face and gnarled hands. He was chewing tobacco, not a common sight in Philly or San Francisco, and he was cheerful. 'Help you folks?'

'Fill it with regular, please,' Alex said, passing his credit card through the window. 'It probably only needs half a tank.'

'Sure thing.' Four letters – CHET – were stitched across the man's shirt pocket. Chet bent down and looked past Alex at the boy. 'How are you, Chief?'

Colin looked at him, incredulous. 'F-f-fine,' he stammered.

Chet showed a mouthful of stained teeth. 'Glad to hear it.' Then he went to the back of the car to put in the gasoline.

'Why did he call me Chief?' Colin asked. He was over his incredulity now, and he was embarrassed instead.

19

'Maybe he thinks you're an Indian,' Alex said.

'Oh, sure.'

'Or in charge of a fire company.'

Colin scrunched down in the seat and looked at him sourly. 'I should have gone on the plane with Courtney. I can't take your bad jokes for five days.'

Alex laughed. 'You're too much.' He knew that Colin's perceptions and vocabulary were far in advance of his real age, and he had long ago grown accustomed to the boy's sometimes startling sarcasm and occasional good turn of phrase. But there was a forced quality to this precocious banter. Colin was trying hard to be grown up. He was straining out of childhood, trying to grit his teeth and *will* his way through adolescence and into adulthood. Doyle was familiar with that temperament, for it had been his own when he was Colin's age.

Chet came back and gave Doyle the credit card and sales form on a hard plastic holder. While Alex took the pen and scrawled his name, the attendant peered at Colin again. 'Have a long trip ahead of you, Chief?'

Colin was as shaken this time as he had been when Chet had first addressed him. 'California,' he said, looking at his knees.

'Well,' Chet said, 'ain't that something. You're the second in an hour on his way to California. I always ask where people's going. Gives me a sense of helping them along, you know? An hour ago this guy's going to California, and now you. Everyone's going to California except me.' He sighed.

Alex gave back the clipboard and tucked his credit card into his wallet. He glanced at Colin and saw that the boy was intently cleaning one fingernail with the other in order to have something to occupy his eyes if Chet should want to resume their one-sided conversation.

'Here you go,' Chet handed Alex the receipt. 'Way out to the coast?' He shifted his wad of tobacco from the left to the right side of his mouth.

'That's right.'

'Brothers?' Chet asked.

'Excuse me?'

'You two brothers?'

'Oh no,' Alex said. He knew there was no time or reason for full explanation of his and Colin's relationship. 'He's my son.'

'Son?' Chet seemed not to have heard the word before.

'Yes.' Even if he was not Colin's father, he was old enough to be.

Chet looked at Doyle's coarse hair, at the way it spilled over his collar. He looked critically at Doyle's brightly patterned shirt with its large wooden buttons. Alex almost thanked the man for implying that he was not old enough to have a son Colin's age – and then he realized that the attendant's mood had changed. The man was not saying Doyle was too young to be father to an eleven-year-old, but that a father ought to set a better example. Doyle could look and dress strangely if he were Colin's brother, but if he were Colin's father, it was inappropriate – at least, it was to Chet's way of thinking.

'Thought you was twenty, twenty-one,' Chet said, tonguing his tobacco.

'Thirty,' Alex said, wondering why he bothered to answer.

The attendant looked at the sleek black car. A subtle hardness came into his eyes. Clearly, he thought that while it was fine for Doyle to be driving a Thunderbird that belonged to his father, it was a different thing if Doyle owned the car himself. If a man who looked like Doyle could have a fancy car and trips to California, while a working man half again his age could not – there was no justice. 'Well,' Alex said, 'have a good day.'

Chet stepped back on to the pump island without wishing them a good trip. He frowned at the car. When the power window hummed up in one smooth motion, he frowned more deeply, the lines in his red brow bunched together like rolls in corrugated sheet metal.

'Such a nice man.' Alex put the car in gear and got out of there.

When they were on the turnpike going west again, Colin suddenly laughed aloud.

'What's so funny?' Alex asked. He was shivering inside, angry with Chet out of proportion to what the man had done. Indeed, the man had done nothing except reveal a rather quiet prejudice.

'When he said you looked twenty-one, I thought he was going to call you Chief like he did me,' Colin said. 'That would have been good.'

'Oh, sure! That would have been just hysterical.'

Colin shrugged. 'You thought it was funny when he called *me* Chief.'

As Doyle's anger and fear settled, he realised that his own reaction to the attendant's unvoiced hatred was only a milder version of that over-reaction which Colin had shown to the man's friendly small talk. Had the boy seen through Chet's original folksy persona to the not-so-folksy core? Or had he just been his usual shy self? It really did not matter. Whatever the case, the fact remained that an injustice had been done both of them. 'I apologise, Colin. I should never have approved of the condescending tone he used with you.'

'He treated me like I was a child.'

'It's a natural trap for adults to fall into,' Alex said. 'But it isn't right. Are you going to accept my apology?'

Colin was especially serious, sitting straight and stiff, for this was the first time an adult had asked his forgiveness. 'I accept,' he said soberly. Then his gamin face broke into a wide smile. 'But I still wish that he had called *you* Chief just like he did me.'

Thick pines and black-trunked elms crowded against the sides of the road now, swaying gently in the spring wind.

The highway rose nearly a mile. At the crest it did not slope down again but continued across a flat table of land towards another gradual slope a mile away. The forest still loomed up, the tall sentinel pines in grand array, the sprawling elms like generals inspecting the troops.

Halfway along this flat stretch, on the right, was a picnic and rest area. The brush had been cleared from beneath the trees. A few wooden tables — anchored to concrete stanchions to guard against theft — and several trash baskets were fixed at intervals under the scattered pines. A sign announced public rest rooms.

At this hour of the morning there was no one at the picnic tables. However, at the far western end of the miniature park, stopped in the exit lane and waiting to pull back onto the pike, was the delivery van.

AUTOMOVER
ONE-WAY MOVE-IT-YOURSELF
CONVENIENCE!

It was unquestionably the same van.

'There he is again!' Colin said, pressing his nose against the window as they swept past the van at seventy miles an hour. 'It really is him!'

Doyle looked in the rear-view mirror and watched the delivery van pull on to the main road. It accelerated rapidly. In three or four minutes it caught up with them, settling in a quarter of a mile behind, pacing them as it had before.

Doyle knew that it was just coincidence. There was no reality in Colin's game. It was as much make-believe as all the games he had played with the boy in the past. No one in the world had a grudge against them. No one in the world had a reason to follow them with sinister intent. Coincidence . . .

Nevertheless, a chill lay the length of his back, a crust of imaginary ice.

Two

George Leland handled the rented twenty-foot Chevrolet van as if he were pushing a baby carriage, not even rattling the furniture and household goods which were packed into the cargo space behind the front seat. The land whizzed past, and the road rumbled underneath, and Leland was in command of it all.

He had grown up with trucks and other big machines, and he had a special talent for making them perform as they had been built to perform. On the farm near Lancaster, he had driven a hay truck by the time he was thirteen, touring his father's fields and loading from the separate baler beds. Before he was out of high school, he had operated the mower, baler, plough, and all the other powerful equipment that brought a farm full circle from planting to harvesting to planting once more. When he went away to college, he helped pay his tuition by driving a delivery van much like the one he was now pushing across Pennsylvania. Later, when he was of age, he drove a full-size rig for a fuel-oil company, and in two summers of that he had not put a single nick on his truck or any passing automobile. He had been offered a job with the oil company after that second summer, but he had turned it down, of course. A year later, when he received his second degree in civil engineering and took his first *real* job, he often hopped up on one of the gigantic earth-moving machines and ran it through its paces – not because he was worried that the job was going badly, but because he enjoyed using the machine, enjoyed knowing that his touch with it was sure.

Now, all Monday morning and then past noon, he nursed the rented van westward. He stayed the same distance behind the black Thunderbird at all times. When the car slowed down, he slowed down too. When it accelerated, he quickly caught up with it. For the most part, however, the Thunderbird maintained a precise seventy miles an hour. Leland knew that the top-of-the line model T-Bird had a speed-set control on the steering wheel which took some of the effort out of long-distance driving. Doyle was probably using that device. But it did not matter. Effortlessly, skilfully, George Leland matched the car's automatically controlled pace for hour after hour, almost as if he were a machine himself.

Leland was a big man, six-three and over two hundred pounds. He had once been twenty pounds heavier, but lately he had suffered a weight loss because he forgot to eat regular meals. His broad shoulders were more hunched than they had been once, his narrow waist even narrower. He had a square face framed with blond, almost white, hair. His eyes were blue, complexion clear except for a spray of freckles across his blunt nose. His neck was all muscle, gristle, and corded veins. When he gripped the steering wheel with his big hands and made his biceps swell with the unconscious fierceness of his grip, he looked absolutely immovable, as if he were welded to the vehicle.

He did not switch on his radio.

He did not look at the scenery.

He did not smoke, chew gum, or talk to himself.

Mile after mile, his attention was on the road, the car ahead, the machine that hummed satisfactorily all around him. Not once in those first hours of the journey did he think specifically about the man and the boy in the Thunderbird. His discordant thoughts, but for his driving, were vague and undetailed. Mostly he was riveted by a broad mesmeric hatred that had no single focus. Somehow the car ahead would eventually become that focus. He knew this. But for the moment he only followed like a machine.

From Harrisburg, the Thunderbird went west on the turnpike, switched from that to Interstate 70, and passed across the northernmost sliver of West Virginia. Past Wheeling, barely inside of Ohio, the car signalled its intention to take an exit lane into a service area full of gasoline stations, motels, and restaurants.

The moment he saw the flashing signal, Leland braked and allowed the van to fall a mile behind Doyle. When he took the ramp a minute after the Thunderbird, the big black car was nowhere in sight. At the bottom of the ramp, Leland hesitated only a second, then turned west towards the heaviest concentration of tourist facilities. He drove slowly, looking for their car. He found it parked in front of a rectangular aluminium diner that looked like an old-fashioned railroad passenger car. The T-Bird was cooling in the shade of a huge sign that proclaimed HARRY'S FINE FOOD.

Leland drove until he came to Breen's, the last diner in the chrome, plastic, fake-stone, neon jungle of the interchange. He parked the Chevrolet on the far side of the small structure so that no one down at Harry's Fine Food, five hundred yards away, would see it. He got out, locked the van and went to have his own lunch.

Breen's was, at least on the outside, much like the restaurant where Doyle and the kid had stopped. It was eighty feet long, an aluminium tube designed to look like a railroad passenger car, with one long narrow window row around three sides and an entrance cubicle tacked on the front almost as an afterthought.

Inside, a single width of cracked plastic-coated booths was built onto the wall beside the contiguous windows. Each booth was equipped with a scarred ashtray, cylindrical glass sugar dispenser, glass salt and pepper shakers, a stainless-steel napkin dispenser, and a selector for the jukebox that stood next to the toilets at the extreme east end of the restaurant. A wide aisle separated the booths from the counter that ran from one end of the place to the other.

Leland turned right when he went in, walked to the end of the counter, and sat on the curve where he could occasionally look out of the windows beyond the booths and see the Thunderbird down at Harry's.

Because it was the last restaurant in the complex, and because the lunch-hour rush had passed by two-thirty in the afternoon, Breen's was almost deserted. In a booth just inside the door, a middle-aged couple worked at hot roast beef sandwiches in mutual stony silence. An Ohio State Police lieutenant occupied the booth behind them, facing Leland. He was busy with a cheeseburger and French fries. In the booth at the far end of the room from Leland, a frowsy waitress with bleached hair smoked a cigarette and stared at the yellowed tile ceiling.

The only other person in the place was the counter waitress, who came to see what Leland wanted. She was perhaps nineteen, a fresh and pretty blonde with eyes as blue as Leland's. Her uniform was off the rack of a discount house, but she had personalised it. The skirt was hemmed eight inches above her shapely knees. A small embroidered chipmunk capered on her skirt pocket, a rabbit on the other. She had replaced the uniform's original white buttons with red ones. On her left breast stood an embroidered bird, and on her right breast was her name in fancy script: *Janet.* And a cheerful greeting just below the name: *Hi there!* She had a sweet smile, a curiously charming way of cocking her head, an almost Mickey Mouse cuteness – and she was obviously an easy lay.

'Seen the menu?' she asked. Her voice was at once throaty and childlike.

'Coffee and a cheeseburger,' Leland said.

'French fries too? They're already made.'

'Well, okay,' he said.

She wrote it all down, then winked at him. 'Back in a jiff.'

He watched her walk up the service aisle behind the counter. Her trim legs scissored prettily. Her tight uniform clung to the well-delineated halves of her round ass. Suddenly, though the transformation was impossible, she was nude. To his eye, her clothes vanished in an instant. He saw all of her long legs, the divided globe of her behind, the exquisite line of her slim back . . .

He looked guiltily down at the counter top as he felt his loins tighten, and he was abruptly confused, disoriented. In that instant he could not even say where he was.

Janet came back with the coffee and put it in front of him. 'Cream?'

'Yes, please.'

She reached under the counter and came up with a two-inch-high cardboard container shaped like a milk bottle. She laid out his silverware, inspected her work, and approved. Instead of leaving him to his coffee, however, she leaned her elbows on the counter, propped her chin in her hands, gave him a saucy grin. 'Where are you moving to?' she asked.

Leland frowned. 'How did you know I'm moving?'

'Saw you pull in. Saw the Automover. You moving around here someplace?'

'No,' he said, pouring cream into his coffee. 'California.'

'Oh wow!' she said. 'Great! Palm trees, sunshine, surfing . . .'

'Yeah,' he said, wishing she would go away.

'I'd love to learn to surf,' she said. 'I like the sea. Summers, I take two weeks in Atlantic City, lay around on the beach and get real brown. I tan well. I have this *very* skimpy bikini that browns me all over.' She laughed with false modesty. 'Well . . . *Almost* all over. They don't approve of bikinis *that* small in Atlantic City.'

Leland looked at her over the rim of his coffee cup.

She met his eyes and held them until he looked down again.

'Burg and fries!' the cook called from the serving window which connected the restaurant to the kitchen.

'Yours,' she said quietly. She went and got the food, put it down before him. 'Anything else?'

'No,' he said.

She leaned against the counter again, talking while he ate. She worked hard at her ingenuousness. She giggled, did a lot of blinking and practised blushing. He decided she was five years older than he had first thought.

'Could I have another cup of coffee?' he asked at last, just to be rid of her for a few moments.

'Sure,' she said, picking up his empty cup and walking back towards the tall chrome brewer.

Watching her, Leland felt an odd vibration pass through him – and then he was seeing her without her clothes just as he had before. He was not just imagining what she would like when she was nude. He actually *saw* her as clearly as he saw the normal features of the diner around her. Her long legs and round buttocks were taut as she stood on her toes to check the filter in the top of the huge pot. When she turned, her breasts swayed, nipples swelling even as he watched.

Closing his eyes, Leland tried desperately to erase the vision. Opening them, he saw that it remained. And second by second, the longer it remained, the stranger he felt.

He closed his hand around the knife she had given him. He lifted the knife and held it before his face and looked at the bright serrated edge. Then the blade softened, diffused, as he looked beyond it to the nude girl walking slowly towards him, walking towards him as if through syrup, her bare breasts moving sensuously with each step . . . He thought of putting the knife between her ribs, deep between them, then twisting it back and forth until she stopped screaming and gave him a rictus of welcome . . .

Then, when she was almost up to him, the overfilled coffee cup balanced carefully in both her slim hands, Leland realized that someone was watching him. He turned slightly on his stool and looked at the middle-aged couple in the booth by the door. The man had a mouthful of food, but he was not chewing it. Cheeks bulging, he was watching Leland, watching the tight expression on Leland's face and the knife held up like a torch in the engineer's big right hand. In the second booth, the policeman had also stopped eating to watch Leland. He was frowning, as if he didn't quite know what to make of the knife.

Leland put the knife down and slid off the stool just as the waitress arrived with the food. He fumbled for his wallet and threw two dollars on the counter.

'You aren't leaving, are you?' she asked. Her voice was faraway and so icy that it made Leland shiver.

He did not answer her. He walked quickly to the door and went outside. The day seemed fiercely bright as he hurried to the van.

Sitting behind the wheel of the Chevrolet, he heard his heart pounding relentlessly against the walls of his chest. He drew breath in great racking sobs and shuddered like a cold, wet dog.

Though she was not in sight now, and though he held his eyes tightly shut, Leland could see the young waitress: her supple body, long bare legs, widely spaced breasts . . . He could see himself leaning into her with the blade, her fair skin parting, could see himself clambering over the counter and taking her right there on the floor. No one would have stopped him, because he would have kept the knife. Everyone would have been afraid. Even the cop. He could have pressed the waitress down on the dirty tiles behind the counter, could have ravaged her as often as he wanted . . .

He thought about the knife and the blood that would have been and about the girl's breasts and the feel of her body moving against him, and he saw the stunned looks the others in the diner would have given him if he had actually done it. And, gradually, the mood left him. His heart grew quiet. His breath came less raggedly than it had.

He raised his head and unexpectedly caught sight of himself in the wide rear-view mirror fixed beside the driver's window. He looked into his own eyes, and for a moment he knew where he

was and what he was doing. Suddenly lucid, he
realized why he was following the Thunderbird,
what he intended to do to the people inside of it.
And he knew it was all wrong. He was sick,
confused, disoriented.

Looking away from his own eyes, sickened by
what he saw in them, he discovered that the cop
had come out of the diner and was walking
towards the van. Irrationally, he was certain the
trooper knew everything. The trooper somehow
knew all that Leland would have liked to do to the
girl and all that he would do to the pair in the
Thunderbird. The trooper knew.

Leland started the van.

The trooper called to him.

Unable to hear what the man said, certain that
he did not *want* to hear it, Leland put the van in
gear and tramped the accelerator.

The cop shouted again.

The truck jerked, slewed sideways, kicking up
loose gravel. Leland eased up on the gas and
settled the machine. He drove out of the lot and
picked up speed going through the clutter of
motels and service stations.

He was breathing hard again. He was
whimpering.

At the east of the complex, he took the entrance
ramp to Interstate 70 much faster than he should
have. He did not check the traffic, but drove
unheedingly on to the throughway. Fortunately,
both westbound lanes were deserted.

Though in the back of his mind Leland knew
that these roads were well patrolled and even
monitored by radar, he let the needle on the

speedometer climb and climb. When it hit close to a hundred, the van trembled slightly and fell into its maximum pace like a thoroughbred into the proper trot.

In the cargo space, the furniture rattled and banged against the walls. A table lamp fell with a crash of broken glass.

Leland looked in the mirror. The cop either had not started after him or had not started quickly enough. The road back there was empty.

Nevertheless, he held the van at a hundred miles an hour. The road roared beneath him. The flat land spun past like rapidly changed stage settings. And little by little the panic died in him. He gradually lost the feeling that everyone was watching him, that everyone's hand was against him, that he was transparent, and that he was being relentlessly pursued by forces connected with but not really identified by that state policeman. As he barrelled westward, he quickly became a part of his machine once more. He guided it with a safe and measured touch. When he had gone seven or eight miles, he let the speed fall back to the legal limit; and even though only minutes had passed since he left the diner, he could not recall what had made him panic in the first place.

However, he suddenly *did* remember Doyle and Colin. The Thunderbird was somewhere behind him, to the east. Perhaps it was still parked in the shadow of that enormous sign at Harry's Fine Food. Even if it were on the road again, Doyle and the kid were miles to the rear, out of sight. Leland did not like that at all.

He let his speed drop even further. As he began to realize that now *they* were following *him*, his ever-present fear took on a familiar rage. The grey road seemed like a tunnel now, a trap with one exit and no way to turn back.

Then, ahead, another rest area loomed on the right, shielded from the highway by a double row of pines. Leland braked and drove in there, went up a slight incline. He parked on the square gravelled plateau, facing the highway so that he could watch the traffic between the thick brown trunks of the trees.

All he had to do now was wait and watch the road. When the Thunderbird passed, he could fall in behind it, catch up to it in two or three minutes. He was enormously relieved.

The trooper was getting out of the patrol car even before George Leland realized that he had driven into the rest area. Leland had been watching the highway beyond the pines for a full five minutes, and he must have been somewhat mesmerized by the bright sunshine and the spurts of west-bound traffic. One moment he thought he was alone – and the next moment he was aware of the Ohio State Police patrol car angled in beside the van. Half in the shadows cast by the pines and half in the slanting sunlight, it looked unreal. The dome light was flashing, though the siren had not been used. The trooper who got out was in his early thirties, sober and hard-jawed. He was the same man who had been taking his lunch in Breen's, the one who had called to Leland outside the little diner.

38

Leland remembered some of the reasons for his previous panic. Again the world appeared to close in on him. Darkness crept up at the corners of his vision, inward-spreading ink stains. He felt bottled up and vulnerable, an easy target for those who meant him harm. These days everyone seemed to be after him. He was always running.

He rolled down his window as the cop approached.

'You alone?' the lieutenant asked, stopping far enough from the van to be out of the way of the door if Leland should suddenly swing it open. He had one hand on the butt of his holstered revolver.

'Alone?' Leland asked. 'Yes, sir.'

'Why didn't you stop when I called to you?'

'Called to me?'

'At the restaurant,' the lieutenant said, his voice crisp and older than his smooth face.

Leland looked perplexed. 'I didn't see you. You called me?'

'Twice.'

'I'm sorry,' Leland said. 'I didn't hear.' He frowned. 'Did I do something wrong? I'm usually a careful driver.'

The trooper watched him carefully for a moment, searched his blue eyes, took in his sun-darkened face and neatly trimmed hair, then relaxed. He let his hand drop from the gun. He took the last few steps to the van. 'It wasn't your driving,' he said. 'Just the same, I'd like to have a look at your licence and the rental papers for the truck.'

'Sure,' Leland said. 'Always glad to cooperate.'

Moving as if he were searching for his wallet, he took the .32-calibre pistol out of the tissue box on the seat beside him. In one fluid movement he raised it to the window and centred the barrel on the trooper's face and pulled the trigger. The single shot echoed in the copse of pines behind the van and slapped sharply across the highway out front.

Leland sat and watched the traffic on the through-way for several minutes before he realized that he ought to conceal the corpse. Any minute someone could pull into the rest area, see the cop sprawled between the patrol car and the van, and run for help. These days everyone was on his tail. He had stayed alive this long only by keeping one step ahead of them. Now was no time to let his thinking get fuzzy.

He pushed open the van door and got out.

The trooper was lying face down in the gravel, dark blood pooled around his head. He looked much smaller now, almost like a child.

During the past year, when he sensed the conspiracy working against him, Leland had wondered whether he would be able to kill to protect himself. He knew it would come to that. Kill or be killed. And until this moment he had not been sure which it would be. Now he could not understand why he had ever been in doubt. When it was kill or be killed, even a non-violent man could act to save himself.

Expressionlessly Leland bent down and grabbed hold of the dead man's ankles, dragged him around to the open door of the squad car. The short-wave radio in there was sputtering noisily. Leland heaved the corpse inside, let it slump over the steering wheel. But that was no good. Even from a distance the man looked dead. Aware that he would have to completely conceal it, Leland pushed the body across the vinyl seat and climbed into the car after it.

He touched the steering wheel, unaware he was leaving fingerprints.

He touched the back of the vinyl seat.

Oblivious to the thickening blood, he bent the dead man's ruined face to his knees, then shoved the compacted hulk onto the floor in front of the passenger's seat.

Inadvertently he touched the window on that side of the car, pressing all five fingers firmly to the glass.

He had to force the corpse to slip halfway back into the cavity beneath the dashboard, but when he was done he was confident that no one would find the body unless they opened the door looking for it.

Climbing out, he touched the bench of the vinyl seat.

He touched the steering wheel again.

He closed the door, fingers clasped around the chrome handle.

It never occurred to him that he ought to take a rag and wipe down everything that he had touched. Already he had half forgotten the dead man crammed in the corner of the official car.

He went back to the van and got in and closed the door. On the highway, traffic flashed by, casting off a golden shower of late-afternoon sunlight. For ten minutes or more Leland watched the road, waiting for the Thunderbird to pass.

With his physical attention focused on so small an area, his thoughts drifted until they eventually settled on the young waitress who had served him at the diner, the girl with the rabbits and chipmunks on her uniform. Now he saw why she had confused and upset him. With her long natural-platinum hair and elfin features, she looked a little bit like Courtney. Not much, but some. Therefore she had precipitated his spell. He knew, now, that he did not want to put a knife into her, had never wanted to put his knife into her. He did not want to make love to her, either. Indeed, he had no interest in that girl at all. He was strictly a one-woman man. He cared only for his lovely Courtney.

As quickly as his thoughts passed from the waitress to Courtney, they flicked from Courtney to Doyle and the boy. Leland was shocked at the suddenly perceived possibility that the Thunderbird had passed while he was putting the dead trooper into the squad car. Perhaps they had gone by twenty minutes ago. They could be miles and miles out in front of him . . .

What if Doyle changed his intended route? What if he did not follow the road that was marked on his map?

Leland felt a hard lump of fear rise in his throat.

If he lost Doyle and the kid, wouldn't he be losing Courtney? If he lost Courtney, lost his way to Courtney, hadn't he then lost everything?

Droplets of sweat standing out on his broad forehead despite the air conditioning, he slipped the van in gear and backed out of there. The front wheels arced through the bloodied gravel. He shifted into drive and took the Chevrolet out of the rest area. The dome light on the squad car still went around and around, but Leland was not aware of that. There was no reality for him except the road ahead and the Thunderbird which must be even now escaping from him.

Three

When they had been back on the road for fifteen
minutes after their lunch break and still the rented
Chevrolet van had not appeared in the rear-view
mirror, Doyle stopped watching for it. He had
been shaken when the van pulled behind them
again after their breakfast stop near Harrisburg,
but of course that had been merely coincidence. It
had trailed them across all of Pennsylvania and
through a sliver of West Virginia, then into Ohio –
but that was because it happened to be going west
on the same Interstate they were using. The driver
of the van, whoever he was, had chosen his route
from a map, just as Doyle had; there was nothing
sinister in the other man's mind when he outlined
his trip. Belatedly Alex realized that he could
have relieved his own mind at any time during
the morning just by pulling to the side of the road
and letting the van go past. He could have waited
for it to build up a fifteen-minute lead and could
have dispensed immediately with the whole crazy
idea that they were being pursued. Well, it did not
matter much now. The van was gone, way out
ahead of them somewhere.

'He back there?' Colin asked.

'No.'

'Shucks.'

'Shucks?'

'I'd really like to know what he was up to,' Colin said. 'Now I guess we'll never find out.'

Alex smiled. 'I guess we never will.'

Compared to Pennsylvania, Ohio was almost a plains state. Vistas of open green land stretched out on both sides of the highway, marred only by an occasional shabby town, neat farm, or oddly isolated and routinely filthy factory. The sameness of it, stretching away into the distance under an equally bland blue sky, bored and depressed them. The car seemed to crawl at a quarter of its real speed.

When they had been on the road only twenty minutes, Colin began to twist and squirm uncomfortably. 'This seatbelt isn't made right,' he told Doyle.

'Oh?'

'I think they made it too tight.'

'It can't be too tight. It's adjustable.'

'I don't know . . .' Colin tested it with both hands.

'You aren't getting out of it with excuses as contrived as that one.'

Colin looked at the open fields, at a herd of fat cows grazing on a hill above a white-and-red barn. 'I didn't know there were so many cows in the world. Ever since we left home I've seen cows everywhere I look. If I see one more cow, I think I might puke.'

'No, you won't,' Alex said. 'I'd make you clean it up.'

'Is the rest of the country going to be like this?'

Colin asked, indicating the mundane landscape with one slim, upturned hand.

'You know it isn't,' Doyle said patiently. 'You'll see the Mississippi River, the deserts, the Rocky Mountains . . . You've taken enough imaginary trips around the world to know it far better than I do.'

Colin quit tugging at his seatbelt when he saw he was not getting anywhere with Doyle. 'By the time we find these *interesting* places, my brain will be all rotten inside. If I watch too much of this *nothing*, I'll turn into a zombie. You know what a zombie's like?' He made a face like a zombie for Doyle's benefit: mouth agape, flesh slack, eyes open wide but taking in nothing.

While he liked Colin and was amused by him, Doyle was also disturbed. He knew that the boy's persistent campaign to be let out of his belt was as much a test of Doyle's talent for discipline as it was an expression of real discomfort. Before Alex had married Courtney, the boy obeyed his sister's suitor as he might his own father. And even when the honeymooners came home to tie up their affairs in Philadelphia, Colin had behaved. But now that he was alone with Doyle and out of his sister's sight, he was testing their new relationship. If he could get away with anything, he would. In that respect, he was the same as all other boys his age.

'Look,' Alex said, 'When you talk to Courtney on the phone tonight, I don't want you complaining about your seatbelt and the scenery. She and I both thought this trip would be good for you. I might as well tell you that we also thought it would let you and me get used to each other, throw us together and smooth out any wrinkles. Now, I won't have you complaining and groaning when we call her from Indianapolis. She's out in San Francisco getting people to put down the carpet, install the curtains, deliver the furniture . . . She has enough on her mind without worrying about you.'

Colin thought about that as they rushed directly westward towards Columbus. 'Okay,' he said at last. 'I surrender. You have nineteen years on me.'

Alex glanced at the boy, who gave him a shy under-the-eyebrows look, and laughed quietly. 'We'll get along. I always thought we would.'

'Tell me one thing,' the boy said.

'What's that?'

'You have nineteen years on me. And – six on Courtney?'

'That's right.'

'Do you make the rules and regulations for Courtney, too?'

'*Nobody* makes rules and regulations for Courtney,' Doyle said.

Colin folded his skinny arms over his chest and nodded smugly. 'That's sure the truth. I'm glad you understand her. I wouldn't give this marriage six months if you thought you could tell Courtney to wear *her* seatbelt.'

On both sides, flat fields spread out. Cows grazed. Scattered puffs of cloud drifted lazily across the open sky.

After a while Colin said, 'I'll bet you half a buck I can estimate how many cars will pass us going east in the next five minutes – and come within ten of the real number.'

'Half a buck?' Alex asked. 'You're on.'

The dashboard clock ticked off the five minutes as they counted the eastbound cars, announcing each one aloud. Colin was only three off his estimate.

'Double or nothing?' the boy asked.

'What have I got to lose?' Alex asked, grinning, his confidence in the trip and himself and the boy now all restored.

They played the game again. Colin's estimate was only four cars off, and he won another fifty cents. 'Double or nothing?' he asked again, rubbing his long-fingered hands together.

'I don't think so,' Alex said suspiciously. 'How'd you manage that?'

'Easy. I counted them to myself for half an hour until I saw what an average five minutes brought. Then I asked you if you wanted to bet.'

'Maybe we ought to take a detour down to Las Vegas,' Alex said. 'I'll just tag along with you in the casinos and do what you tell me.'

Colin was so pleased by the compliment that he could not think of anything to say. He hugged himself and dropped his head, then looked out the side window and smiled toothily at his own vague reflection in the glass.

Although the boy was not aware of it, Doyle could see that reflection when he took a quick look at Colin to see why he had become silent so suddenly. Understanding, he grinned himself and relaxed against the seat, the last bit of tension draining out of him. He saw that he had not fallen in love with one person, but with two. He loved this skinny, overly-intellectual boy almost as much as he loved Courtney. It was the sort of realization that could make a man forget the uncertainty and shallow, disquieting fear of the morning.

When he originally mapped the trip and called ahead from Philly to make reservations, and again when he mailed the room-deposit cheque four days ago, Doyle had told the people at the Lazy Time Motel that he and Colin would arrive between seven and eight o'clock Monday evening. At seven-thirty, precisely in the middle of his estimate, he drove into the motel's lot, just east of Indianapolis, and parked by the office.

Their rooms were reserved ahead for the entire trip. Doyle did not want to drive six hundred miles only to spend half the night looking for a vacancy.

He shut off the headlights, then the car. The silence was eerie. Gradually the traffic sounds from the Interstate came to him, forlorn cries on the early-night air. 'How's this for a schedule?' he asked Colin. 'A hot shower, a good supper. Then we call Courtney – and hit the sack for eight hours.'

'Sure,' Colin said. 'But could we eat first?'

The request was an unusual one for him. He was as light an eater as Doyle had been at his age. When they had stopped for lunch today, Colin nibbled at one piece of chicken, ate some cole slaw, a dish of sherbet, drank a Coke – then proclaimed himself 'stuffed'.

'Well,' Doyle said, 'we're not so grubby they'll refuse to let us in the restaurant. But I want to get our rooms first.' He opened his door and let the chill but muggy night air into the car. 'You wait here for me.'

'Sure,' Colin said. 'If I can get out of the seatbelt now.'

Alex smiled, unfastened his own belt. 'I really scared you, did I?'

Colin gave him a lopsided smile. 'If you want to look at it that way.'

'Okay, okay,' Doyle said. 'Take off your seat-belt, Colin me boy.'

When he got out of the car and stretched his legs, he saw that the Lazy Time Motel was just what the tour-guide book said it was: clean, pleasant, but inexpensive. It was built as a large L, with the neon-framed office at the junction of the two wings. Forty or fifty doors, all alike and spaced as evenly as the slats in a fence, were set into undistinguished red-brick walls. A concrete promenade fronted both wings and was covered by a corrugated aluminium awning supported by black wrought-iron posts every ten feet. A soda machine stood just outside the office door, humming and clinking to itself.

The office was small, but the walls were bright yellow, the tile floors clean and polished. Doyle crossed to the counter and struck the bell for service.

'Just a *minute!*' a woman called from behind a bamboo-curtained doorway at the end of the work area on the business side of the counter.

Beside the counter was a rack of magazines and

paperback books. A sign above the rack read:
TONIGHT, WHY NOT READ YOURSELF TO SLEEP?
While Doyle waited for the clerk, he looked at the
books, though he would not need anything to
make him sleepy after all day on the road.

'Sorry to make you wait,' she said, shouldering
through the bamboo curtain. 'I was—' Halfway
from the curtain to the counter, she got a look at
Doyle, and she stopped talking. She stared at him
the same way Chet, at the service station, had
stared. 'Yes?' Her voice was decidedly cool.

'You've got reservations for Doyle,' Alex said.
Now he was doubly glad he had made reservations. He was fairly sure she would have turned
him away, even if he could see there was not a car
in front of every room and even if the neon
vacancy sign *was* lighted.

'Doyle?' she asked.

'Doyle.'

She came the rest of the way to the counter,
brightened as she reached for the file cards by the
registry book. 'Oh, the father and son from
Philadelphia!'

'That's right,' Doyle said, trying to smile.

She was in her middle fifties, an attractive
woman despite the extra twenty pounds she
carried. She wore her hair in a 1950's bouffant,
her broad forehead revealed, spit curls at her ears.
Her knit dress clung to a full if matronly bosom.
The lines of a girdle showed at hips and waist.

'That was one of our seventeen-dollar rooms,'
she said.

'Yes.'

She took the file card from the green metal box,

looked closely at it, then flipped open the registration book. She carefully completed a third-of-a-page form, then turned the book around and held out the pen. 'If you'll sign here . . . Oh,' she said as he reached for the pen, 'maybe your father should sign. The room *is* reserved in his name.'

Doyle looked at her uncomprehendingly until he realized she had more in common with Chet than he had first thought. 'I *am* the father. I'm Alex Doyle.'

She frowned. When she tilted her head, the bouffant seemed about to slide right down over her face in one well-sprayed piece. 'But it says here—'

'My boy's eleven.' He took the pen and scribbled his signature on the form.

She looked at the freshly inked name as if it were an ugly spot on her new slipcovers. Any minute now she would run for the solvent and scrub the nasty thing away.

'Which room have we got?' Alex asked, prodding her along against her will.

She took in his hair and clothes again. He was not accustomed to such frank disapproval in cities like Philly and San Francisco, and he resented her manner.

'Well,' she said, 'you must be aware that you pay—'

'In advance,' he finished for her. 'Yes, silly of me not to think of it.' He counted twelve dollars on to the registration book. 'I sent in a five-dollar deposit, you may recall.'

'But there's tax,' she said.

'How much?'

When she told him, he paid from the loose change in the pocket of his wrinkled dark-grey jeans.

She counted the money into the cash drawer even though she had seen him count it himself a minute ago. Reluctantly she took a key from the pegboard and gave it to him. 'Room 37,' she said, staring at the key as if it were diamond jewellery she was committing to his care. 'That's way down the long wing.'

'Thank you,' he said, hoping to avoid a scene. He walked back across the clean, well-lighted room towards the door.

'The Lazy Time has very nice rooms,' she said as he reached the door.

He looked back. 'I'm sure it does.'

'We like to keep them that way,' she said.

He nodded grimly and got the hell out of there.

Despite the fact that he had lost sight of the Thunderbird, George Leland began to calm down. For fifteen minutes he pushed the van along at top speed, desperately surveying the traffic ahead for a glimpse of the big car. But his natural empathy with machines acted as a sedative. The fear left him. He let the van slow down. With a growing confidence in his ability to catch up with the Thunderbird, he drove only a few miles an hour over the speed limit. Like a man in a light trance, he was aware only of the road and of the Chevy's engine revving at just the right pitch, and he was considerably quieted by these things.

For the first time all day Leland smiled. And he

wished, for the first time in a long time, that he
had someone to whom he could talk . . .

'You look happy, George,' she said, startling him.

He glanced away from the road.

She was sitting in the passenger's seat, only a
couple of feet away from him. But how was that
possible?

'Courtney,' he said, voice a dry whisper. 'I . . .'

'It's nice to see you so happy,' she said. 'You're
usually so sober.'

He looked back at the road, confused.

But his eyes were drawn to her magnetically an
instant later. The sunlight pierced the windshield
and passed through her as if she were a spirit. It
touched her golden hair and skin, then kept right
on going. He could see the door panel on the
other side of her. He could see through her lovely
face to the window behind her head and the
countryside beyond the window — as if she were
transparent. He could not understand. How could
she be here? How could she know that he was
following Doyle and the boy?

A horn blared nearby.

Leland looked up, surprised to find he had
drifted out of the right lane and almost collided
with a Pontiac trying to pass him. He wheeled
hard right and brought the van back into line.

'How have you been, George?' she asked.

He looked at her, then quickly back at the
highway. She was wearing the same outfit she
had worn when he saw her last: clunky shoes, a
short white skirt, fancy red blouse with long
pointed collar. When he followed her to the
airport a week ago and watched her board the

707, he had been so excited by the way she looked in that trim little suit that he had wanted her more than he had ever wanted a woman before. He almost rushed up to her – but he had realized that she would think it was strange of him to be following her.

'How have you been, George?' she asked again.

She had been worried about his problems even before he recognized that he had any, even before he had seen that everything was going wrong. When she dissolved their two-year-old affair and would only talk to him on the telephone, she had still called him twice a month to see how he was getting along. Of course, she had stopped calling eventually. She had forgotten him completely.

'Oh,' he said, keeping his eyes on the road. 'I'm fine.'

'You don't look fine.' Her voice was faraway, hollow, only slightly like her real voice. Yet there she was, sitting beside him in broad daylight.

'I'm doing very well,' he assured her.

'You've lost weight.'

'I needed to lose some.'

'Not *that* much, George.'

'It can't hurt.'

'And you have bags under your eyes.'

He took one hand from the wheel and touched the discoloured, puffy flesh.

'Haven't you been getting enough sleep?' she asked.

He did not respond. He did not like this conversation. He hated her when she badgered him about his health and said his emotional problems with other people must come from a basic *physical* illness. Sure, the problem had come on suddenly. But he wasn't at fault. It was other people. Lately, everyone had it in for him.

'George, have people been treating you better since we last talked?'

He admired her long legs. They were not transparent now. The flesh was golden, firm, beautiful. 'No, Courtney. I lost another job.'

Now that she had stopped nagging him about his health, he felt better. He wanted to tell her everything, no matter how embarrassing. She would understand. He would put his head in her lap and cry until he had no tears left. Then he would feel better . . . He would cry while she smoothed his hair, and when he sat up he would have as few problems as he had had more than two years ago, before this trouble had come along and everyone had gotten nasty with him.

'Another job?' she asked. 'How many jobs have you held these last two years?'

'Six,' he said.

'What did you get fired for this time?'

'I don't know,' Leland said, genuine misery in his voice. 'We were putting up an office building – two years of work. I was getting along with everyone. Then my boss, the chief engineer, started in on me.'

'Started in on you?' she asked, flat and far away, barely audible above the buzz of the wide tyres. 'How?'

He shifted uneasily behind the wheel. 'You know, Courtney. Just like all the other times. He talked about me behind my back, set the other men against me. He countermanded my job

57

assignments and encouraged Preston, the steel foreman, to—'

'He did all this behind your back?' she asked.

'Yes. He—'

'If he said all this behind your back, how do you really know he said anything at all?' He could not tolerate the sympathy in her voice, for it was too much like pity. 'Did you hear him? You didn't hear him yourself, did you, George?'

'Don't talk to me like that. Don't try to say it was my imagination.'

She was quiet, as ordered.

He looked to see if she was still there. She smiled at him, more solid than she had been a few minutes ago.

He looked at the setting sun, but did not see it. He was now only minimally conscious of the highway ahead. Unsettled by her magical presence, he no longer handled the Chevrolet van as well as he could. It drifted back and forth within the right-hand lane, now and then running on to the gravel shoulder.

After a while he said, 'Did you know that after I called you that day just to ask for a date, after I found you were already three weeks married – I almost went out of my mind? I followed you for a week, day in and day out, just watching you. Did you know? You had said you were flying to Frisco, that this man Doyle and your brother would follow in a week, and you said you didn't think you'd ever come back to Philly again. That nearly killed me, Courtney. Everything was going so badly for me. I remembered how good we had it once . . . So I called to see if maybe we could get together again. I was going to ask for a date. Did you know that? You didn't, I'll bet. I was all ready to ask for a date . . . And then I find out you're married and running clear across country.' His voice got hard, cold, almost mean. He paused to collect his thoughts. 'You were my good luck – two, three, four years ago. When we were together, everything was fine. Now you're going to be out of touch, out of sight . . . I knew I had to be near you, Courtney. When I followed you to the airport and saw you leave on that 707, I knew I'd have to follow Doyle and Colin and find out where you were living.'

She said nothing.

He drove and talked on, hoping to get a positive reaction from her, no longer perplexed by her sudden appearance. 'I had lost my job again. There was nothing to keep me in Philly. Of course, I didn't have money to pay movers like this Doyle did. I had to pack and haul my own things. So I'm driving this clumsy van with its poor air conditioning instead of a fancy Thunderbird. I'm not having a run of luck like this Doyle of yours. People aren't treating me as well as they're treating him. But I knew I had to come out to California anyway, to be near you. To be near you, Courtney . . .'

Pretty, quiet, unmoving, she sat there, her slim hands folded in her lap, a nimbus of the day's last light encircling her head.

'It wasn't easy staying on their trail,' he told her. 'I had to be smart. When they were eating breakfast, I realized they must have a marked map in the car, something that would show me which way they were going. I checked.' He gave her a quick glance, grinning, looked at the road again. 'I put a wire coat hanger through the rubber seal between the windows and popped the lock button. The maps were on the seat. An address book, too. Your man Doyle is extremely efficient. He'd written down the names and addresses of the motels where he had reservations. I copied them. And I studied the maps. I know every road they're taking and every place they'll stay over-night between here and San Francisco. Now I can't lose them. I'll just trail along behind. I don't have them in sight this minute, but I'll connect with them later.' He talked very fast, running his words together. He was eager for her to under-stand the trouble he had gone to so that he might be near her.

She surprised him. 'George, did you ever see a doctor about your headaches, about your other problems?'

'I'm not sick, damn you!' he shouted. 'I've got a healthy mind, healthy brain, healthy body. I'm in good shape. I don't want to hear anything more about that. Just forget about that.'

'*Why* are you following them?' she asked, changing the subject as ordered.

Perspiration ran off his brow in several steady streams, fat crystal droplets that tickled his cheeks and neck. 'Didn't I just tell you? I wanted to find out where you'll be living. I want to be near you.'

'But if you copied the addresses in Alex's book, you have our new home address in San Fran-cisco. You don't have to follow them to find me. You already know where I am, George.'

'Well . . .'

'George, *why* are you following Alex and Colin?'

'I told you.'

'You did not.'

'Shut up!' he said. 'I don't like what you're implying. I won't listen to any more of this. I'm healthy. I'm not sick. There's nothing at all wrong with me. So just go away. Leave me alone. I don't want to have to look at you.'

The next time he looked, she was gone. She had vanished.

Although he had been momentarily confused by her unexpected and unexplained appearance, he was not at all surprised by her disappearance. He had *told* her to go away. Towards the end of their affair, just before she broke off with him two years ago, Courtney had said that he frightened her, that these recent black moods of his made her uneasy. She was still scared of him. When he said 'Go', she went. She knew better than to argue. The thoughtless bitch had betrayed him by marrying this Doyle, and now she would do anything to stay in his good graces.

He smiled at the darkening highway.

In the last light of day, with the land drenched in an almost eerie orange radiance, Ohio State Police officer Eric James Coffey drove off Interstate 70 in a picnic and rest area on the right-hand side of the road. He went up the slight incline to the pine-shielded clearing, and he saw the empty squad car at once. The dome light still swivelled, transmitting a red pulse to the trees on all sides.

Since four o'clock, when Lieutenant Richard Pulham had been one hour late returning his cruiser to the division garage at the end of his shift, more than twenty of his fellow troopers had been scouring the Interstate and all the secondary access roads leading to and from it. And now Coffey had found the car – identified it by the numerals on the front door – at the extreme west end of Lieutenant Pulham's patrol circuit.

Coffey wished he had not been the one to find it, for he suspected what he would discover. A dead cop. So far as Coffey could see, there was no other possibility.

He picked up the microphone, thumbed the button. 'This is 166, Coffey. I've found our cruiser.' He repeated the message and gave his position to the dispatcher. His voice was thick and quavery.

Reluctantly he shut off the engine and got out of his own car.

The evening air was chilly. A wind had sprung up from the northwest.

'Lieutenant Pulham! Rich Pulham!' he shouted. The name came back to him in whispered imitations of his own voice. He received no other answer.

Resignedly Coffey went to Pulham's cruiser, bent and stared into the passenger's window. With the sun down, the car was full of shadows.

He opened the door. The interior light came on, weak and insufficient because the dome flasher had nearly drained the battery. Still, dim as it was, it illuminated the blackening blood and the body jammed rudely into the space before the front seat.

'Bastards,' Coffey said quietly. 'Bastards, bastards, bastards.' His voice rose with each repetition. 'Cop killers,' he told the onrushing darkness. 'We'll get the sons of bitches.'

Their room at the Lazy Time Motel was large and comfortable. The walls were an off-white colour, the ceiling a couple of feet higher than it would be in any motel built since the end of the fifties. The furniture was heavy and utilitarian, though not spartan by any means. The two easy chairs were well padded and upholstered, and the desk, if surfaced with plastic, gave plenty of knee room and working space. The two double beds were firm, the sheets crisp and redolent of soap and softener. The scarred mahogany nightstand between the beds held a Gideon Bible and a telephone.

Doyle and Colin sat on separate beds, facing each other across the narrow walk space between them. By mutual agreement, Colin was the first to talk to his sister. He held the receiver in both hands. His thick eyeglasses had slipped down his nose and now rested precariously on the very tip of it, though the boy did not seem to notice. 'We were followed all the way from Philadelphia!' he told Courtney as soon as she came on the line.

Alex grimaced.

'A man in a Chevrolet van,' Colin said. 'No. We couldn't get a look at him. He was much too smart for that.' He told her all about their imaginary FBI man. When he tired of that, he told her how he had won a dollar from Doyle. He listened to her

63

for a moment, laughed. 'I tried, but he wouldn't make any more bets.'

Listening to the boy's half of the conversation, Doyle was momentarily jealous of the warm, intimate relationship between Courtney and Colin. They were entirely at ease with each other, and neither one needed to pretend – or disguise – his love. Then the envy passed as Doyle realized his own relationship with Courtney was much the same – and that he and the boy would soon be as close as they both were to the woman.

'She says I'm costing you too much,' Colin said, passing the receiver to Doyle.

He took it. 'Courtney?'

'Hi, darling.' Her voice was rich and full. She might have been beside him instead of at the other end of twenty-five hundred miles of telephone wire.

'Are you okay?'

'Lonely,' she said.

'Not for long. How's the house coming?'

'The carpets are all down.'

'No hassles?'

'Not until the bill arrives,' she said.

'Painters?'

'Been and gone.'

'Then you just have the furniture deliveries to worry about,' he said.

'I can't *wait* for our bedroom suite to get here.'

'Every bride's greatest concern,' he said.

'That's not what I mean, sexist. It's just that this damn sleeping bag gives me a backache.'

He laughed.

'And,' she said, 'have you ever tried camping

out in the middle of an empty, lushly carpeted twenty-by-twenty master bedroom? It's eerie.'

'Maybe we should have all flown out,' Alex said. 'Maybe a furnitureless house would be easier to endure if you had company.'

'No,' she said. 'I'm OK. I just like to gripe. How are you and Colin getting along?'

'Famously,' he said, watching Colin as the boy pushed his glasses up on his pug nose.

'What about this guy following you in the Automover?' she asked.

'It's nothing.'

'One of Colin's games?'

'That's all,' he assured her.

'Hey, did he really take you for a dollar?'

'He really did. He's a sneaky kid. He's a lot like you.'

Colin laughed.

'How's the car handling?' Courtney asked. 'Is six hundred miles a day too much for you, by yourself?'

'Not at all,' he said. 'My back's probably not aching as much as yours. We'll be able to stay right on schedule.'

'I'm glad to hear you say that. I'm a little bit of a sexist myself – and I can't wait to get you in that new bed.'

'Likewise,' he said, smiling.

'I've had several nights to appreciate the view from this damn bedroom window,' she said. 'It's even more spectacular tonight than it was last night. You can see the city lights on the bay, all distorted and glimmering.'

'I'm homesick for a home I've never slept in,'

Doyle said. He was also lovesick, and he was made more feverish by the sound of her voice.

'I love you,' she said.

'Likewise.'

'Say it.'

'I've got an audience,' Doyle said, looking at Colin. The boy was listening, rapt, as if he could hear both sides of the conversation.

'Colin won't be embarrassed by that,' she said. 'Love doesn't embarrass him at all.'

'Okay,' he said. 'I love you.'

Colin grinned and hugged himself.

'Call tomorrow night.'

'As scheduled,' he promised.

'Say goodnight to Colin for me.'

'I will.'

'Goodbye, darling.'

'Goodbye, Courtney.'

He missed her so profoundly that breaking the connection was a little bit like drawing a sharp knife across his own flesh.

When George Leland pulled the rented Chevrolet van into the macadamed lot in front of the Lazy Time Motel, the NO VACANCY sign was on, large green neon letters. He was not disturbed by that, for he had never intended to stay there. He was not as flush as Alex Doyle, not as lucky; he was unable to afford even the Lazy Time's prices. He just drove slowly along the short arm of the L, then down the long branch until he saw the Thunderbird.

He smiled, satisfied with himself. 'Just like in the address book,' he said. 'Doyle, you're nothing if not efficient.'

He drove away from the Lazy Time, then, before he might be seen. He went on down the road, past two dozen other motels, some of them like the Lazy Time and some much fancier. At last he came to a shabby wooden motel with a small vacancy sign out front and a spare, undecorated neon sign at the entrance: DREAMLAND. It looked like an eight-dollar-a-night dive. He drove in and parked near the office.

He rolled down the window and turned the rear-view mirror so that he could get a look at himself. As he took his comb from his pocket, he noticed several dark streaks on his face. He rubbed at the stains, sniffed the residue, then put it to his tongue. Blood. Surprised, he opened the door and examined himself in the glow of the ceiling light. Dried blood was spattered over his trousers and smeared all over his short-sleeved shirt. The soft white hairs on his left arm were now stiff and purple with dried blood.

Where had it come from?

And when?

He knew he had not hurt himself, yet he could not understand whose blood this was if not his own. Thinking about it, he sensed the approach of one of his fierce migraine headaches. Then, in the back of his mind, something ugly stirred and turned over heavily; and although he still could not recall whose blood had been spilled on him, he knew that he dared not attempt to rent a room for the night while he was wearing the stuff.

Praying that his headache would hold off for a while, he readjusted the mirror, closed the door, started the truck, and drove away from the motel. He went half a mile down the road and parked in front of an abandoned service station. He opened his suitcase and took out a change of clothes. He undressed, washed his face and hands with paper tissues and his own spittle, then put on the clean clothes.

He still felt travel-weary and headachy, but he was now presentable enough to face the night clerk at the motel.

Fifteen minutes later he was in his room in Dreamland. It was not much of a room. Ten-foot square, with a tiny attached bath, it seemed more like a place where a man was *put* than like one to which he went voluntarily. The walls were a dirty yellow, scarred, finger-stained, even marked with dust webs in the high corners. The easy chair was new and functional yet ancient. The desk was green tubular steel with a Masonite work surface darkened with the wormlike marks of cigarette burns. The bed was narrow, soft, the sheets patched.

George Leland did not really notice the condition of the room. It was merely a place to him, like any other place.

At the moment he was chiefly concerned with staving off the headache which he could feel building behind his right eye. He dropped his suitcase at the foot of the sagging bed and stripped out of his clothes. In the tiny bathroom's bare shower stall, he let the spray of hot water sluice the weariness from him. For long minutes he stood with the water drumming pleasantly against the back of his skull and neck, for he had found that this would, on rare occasions, lessen the severity of and even cure altogether an oncoming migraine.

This time, however, the water did no good. When he towelled off, all the warning signs of the migraine were still there: dizziness, a pinpoint of bright light whirling round and round and growing larger behind his right eye, clumsiness, a faint but persistent nausea . . .

He remembered that he had skipped breakfast and supper and had taken only half a lunch in-between. Perhaps the headache was caused by hunger. He was not hungry – or at least he did not suffer the pangs of his unconscious self-denial. Nevertheless, he dressed and went outside, where he bought food from vending machines by the pay telephones in the motel's badly lighted breezeway. He dined on two bottles of Coke, a package of peanut-butter crackers, and a Hershey Bar with almonds.

He suffered the headache anyway. It pulsed out from the core of him, rhythmic waves of pain that forced him to be perfectly still lest he make the agony unbearable. Even when he lifted a hand to his forehead, the responding thunder of pain brought him close to the edge of delirium. He stretched out on his bed, flat on his back, twisting the grey sheets in both big hands, and after a while he was not merely approaching the edge of delirium but had leapt deep into it. For more than two hours he lay as rigid as a wooden construc-tion, perspiration rolling off him like moisture from an icy cold water glass. Exhausted, wrung dry, moaning softly, he eventually passed from a

half-aware trance into a troubled but comparatively painless sleep.

As always, there were nightmares. Grotesque
images flickered through his shattered mind like
visions formed at the bottom of a satanic kaleido-
scope, each independent of the other, each a
horrifying minim to recall later: long slender
knives dripping blood into a woman's cupped
palm, maggots crawling in a corpse, enormous
breasts enfolding him and smothering him in a
damp warm sexless caress, acres of scuttling
cockroaches, herds of watchful red-eyed rats
waiting to leap upon him, bloody lovers writhing
ecstatically on a marble floor, Courtney nude and
writhing on a bloody floor, a revolver snapping
bullets into a woman's slim stomach . . .

The nightmares passed. Soon after, sleep passed
as well. Leland groaned and sat up in bed, held
his head in both hands. The headache was gone,
but the memory of it was a new agony. After-
wards he always felt crushingly helpless, vulnerable. And lonely. Lonelier than a man could
endure to be.

'Don't feel lonely,' Courtney said. 'I'm here with
you.'

Leland looked up and saw her sitting on the
foot of the bed. This time he was not the least bit
surprised by her magical materialization. 'It was
so bad, Courtney,' he said.

'Headache?'

'And nightmares.'

'Did you ever go back to Dr Penebaker?' she
asked.

'No.'

Her gentle voice came to him as if she were speaking from the far end of a tunnel. The hollow, distant tone was curiously in harmony with the shabby room. 'You should have let Dr Penebaker—'

'I don't want to *hear* about Penebaker!'

She said nothing more.

Several minutes later he said, 'I stood by you when your parents were killed in the accident. Why didn't you stand by *me* when things first started to go sour?'

'Don't you remember what I told you then, George? I would have stood by you, if you had been willing to get help. But when you refused to admit that your headaches and your emotional problems might be caused by some—'

'Oh, for Christ's sake, shut up! Shut up! You're a rotten, nagging, holier-than-thou bitch, and I don't want to listen to you.'

She did not vanish, but neither did she speak again.

Quite some time later he said, 'We could have it as good as it once was, Courtney. Don't you agree?' He wanted her to agree more than he had ever wanted anything else.

'I agree, George,' she said.

He smiled. 'It could be just like it was. The only thing that's really keeping us apart is this Doyle. And Colin, too. You were always closer to Colin than to me. If Doyle and Colin were dead, I'd be all you had. You would have to come back to me, wouldn't you?'

'Yes,' she said, just as he wanted her to say.

'We'd be happy again, wouldn't we?'

71

'Yes.'

'You'd let me touch you again.'

'Yes, George.'

'Let me sleep with you again.'

'Yes.'

'Live with me?'

'Yes.'

'And people would stop being nasty to me.'

'Yes.'

'You're my lucky piece, always were. With you back, it would almost be as if the last two years never even happened.'

'Yes,' she said.

But it was no good. She was not as responsive and warm and open as he would have liked. Indeed, talking with her was almost like talking with himself, a curiously masturbatory enterprise.

Angry with her, he turned away and refused to talk any more. A few minutes later, when he looked back to see if she was showing any signs of contrition, he found that she had vanished. She had left him again. She was always leaving him. She was always going away to Doyle or Colin or somebody else and leaving him alone. He did not think that he could tolerate much more of that sort of treatment.

A police cruiser blocked the entrance to the rest area off Interstate 70, dome light and emergency blinkers flashing. Behind it, up on the clearing in the shelter of the pines, half a dozen other official cars were parked in a semicircle with their headlights on and engines running. Several portable kliegs had been hooked up to auxiliary batteries and arranged in another semicircle at the south edge of the clearing, facing the automobiles. In that vicinity, at least, night did not exist.

The focus of all this was, of course, Lieutenant Pulham's cruiser. The bumpers and chrome trim glinted with cold, white light. In the glare, the windshield had been transformed into a mirror.

Detective Ernie Hoval, who was in charge of the Pulham investigation, watched a lab technician photograph the five bloody fingerprints which were impressed so clearly on the inside of the right front car windows, hundreds of fine red whorls. 'They Pulham's prints?' he asked the lab man when the last of the shots had been aligned and taken.

'I'll check in a minute.' The technician was thin, sallow, balding, with hands as delicate and soft as a woman's. Yet he apparently was not intimidated by Hoval. Everyone else was. Hoval used both his rank and his two hundred and forty pounds to dominate everyone who worked under him, and he was annoyed with the technician when the man failed to be impressed. The soft white hands packed the camera away with deliberately maddening care. Only when that was all secured as it should be, did they pick through the other contents of the leather satchel beside the squad car and come up with file copies of Lieutenant Pulham's fingerprints. The technician raised the yellow sheet and held it beside the bloody prints on the window.

'Well?' Hoval asked.

The lab man took a full minute, studying the

two sets of prints. 'They aren't Pulham's,' he said at last.

'Son of a bitch,' Hoval said, slamming one meaty fist into the other open palm. 'It's going to be easier than I thought.'

'Not necessarily.'

Hoval looked down at the pale, narrow man. 'Oh?'

The technician got to his feet and dusted his hands together. He noticed that in the crossglare of all the lights, neither he nor Hoval nor any of the others cast a shadow. 'Not everyone in the United States has his prints on file,' the technician said. 'Far less than half of us, in fact.'

Hoval gestured impatiently with one strong hand. 'Whoever did this is on file, believe me. Probably arrested in a dozen different protest marches – maybe even on a previous assault charge. FBI probably has a full file on him.'

The lab man wiped one hand across his face, as if he were trying to pull away his perpetually sorrowful expression. 'You think it was a radical, a new leftist, somebody like that?'

'Who else?' Hoval asked.

'Maybe just a nut.'

Hoval shook his square, long-jawed head. 'No. Don't you read the papers any more? Policemen getting killed all over the country these days.'

'It's the nature of their job,' the technician said. 'Policemen have always gotten killed in the line of duty. Percentage of deaths is still the same as it always was.'

Hoval was adamant as he watched the other lab men and the uniformed troopers comb the murder site. 'These days there's an organized effort to slaughter policemen. Nationwide conspiracy. And it's finally touched us. You wait and see. This asshole's prints will be on file. And he'll be just the kind of bastard I'm telling you he is. We'll have him nailed to a post in twenty-four hours.'

'Sure,' the technician said. 'That'll be nice.'

Tuesday

Four

On the second day of May they rose early and ate a light breakfast, checked out of the Lazy Time Motel, and were on the road again shortly after eight o'clock.

The day was as bright and fresh as the previous one had been. The sky was high and cloudless. The sun, behind them once more, seemed to propel them on toward the coast.

'Does the scenery get better today?' Colin asked.

'Some,' Alex said. 'For one thing, you'll get to see the famous Gateway Arch in St Louis.'

'How many miles to St Louis?'

'Oh . . . maybe two-fifty.'

'And this Gateway Arch is the very first thing that we have to look forward to?'

'Well—'

'Christ,' the boy said, shaking his head sorrowfully, 'this is going to be a long, *long* morning.'

Interstate 70 took them west-southwest towards the border of Illinois, a straight multi-lane avenue carved out of the flatlands of America. It was a convenient, fairly safe, controlled access throughway made for fast travel, designed for a nation always in a hurry. Though Doyle was, himself, in a hurry, anxious to be with Courtney again, he shared some of Colin's dissatisfaction with their route. Though simple and quick, it was characterless.

Fields of spring wheat, short and tender and green, began to fill the open spaces on both sides of the highway. Initially, these crisp green vistas and the complex of irrigation pipelines that sprayed them proved moderately interesting. Before too long, however, the fields grew boringly repetitious.

Despite his professed pessimism about the long morning which lay ahead of them, Colin was in a particularly garrulous mood, and he made their first two hours on the road pass most pleasantly and swiftly. They talked about what it would be like to live in California, talked about space travel, astronauts, science fiction, rock-and-roll, pirates, sailing ships, and Count Dracula – this last, chiefly because Colin was wearing a green-and-black Count Dracula T-shirt today, his narrow chest gruesomely decorated with a menacing, fierce-eyed, fanged Christopher Lee.

As they passed the Indiana-Illinois border, there was a lull in the conversation, at last. With Doyle's permission, Colin unbuckled his seatbelt long enough to slide forward and locate a new radio station.

To make certain that nothing was coming up on them too fast while the boy was in such a vulnerable position on the edge of the seat, Alex looked in the rear-view mirror at the light flow of traffic on the broad throughway behind them.

That was when he saw the Chevrolet van.

He looked quickly away from it, looked at the road ahead.

At first he did not want to believe what he had seen, he was sure it must be his imagination. Then he argued with himself that since there were thousands of Automovers on the roads of America, this was most likely *another* of them, not at all the same vehicle that had hung behind them on the first leg of the journey.

Colin slid back on to his seat and buckled his seatbelt without argument. As he carefully smoothed down his T-shirt, he said, 'Is that one okay?'

'What one?'

Colin tilted his head and stared curiously at Doyle. 'The radio station, naturally. What else?'

'Sure. It's fine.'

But Alex was so distracted that he was not actually aware of what sort of music the boy had selected for them. Reluctantly he glanced at the rear-view mirror a second time.

The Automover was still cruising in their wake, no mere figment of his overworked imagination to be lightly dismissed, hanging back there a little less than a quarter of a mile, well silhouetted in the morning sun, nevertheless darkly sinister.

Unaccountably, Doyle thought of the service station attendant whom they had encountered near Harrisburg, and of the stout anachronism behind the desk of the Lazy Time Motel. That familiar and uncontrollable shudder, the embarrassment of his childhood which he had never fully outgrown, started in his stomach and bowels and seemed to generate, of itself, a quiet and possibly irrational fear. However, deep down inside, Doyle admitted to himself what he had been first forced to face up to more than twenty years ago: he was an unmitigated coward. His pacifism was not based on any real moral precepts, but on an abiding terror of violence. When you really thought about it, what danger did that van pose? What injury or threat of injury had it done? If it seemed sinister, the blame was in his own mind. His fear was not only irrational, it was premature and simple-minded. He had no more cause to be frightened by the Chevrolet than he had had to be frightened by Chet or the woman at the Lazy Time.

'He's back there again, isn't he?' Colin said.

'Who?'

'Don't play dumb with me,' the boy said.

'Well, there *is* an Automover behind us.'

'It's him, then.'

'Could be another one.'

'That's too coincidental,' Colin said, quite sure of himself.

For a long moment Doyle was silent. Then: 'Yes, I'm afraid you're right. That's too coincidental. He's behind us again, all right.'

Five

'I'm going to pull over and stop on the shoulder of the road,' Alex said, lightly pumping the power brakes.

'Why?'

'To see what he does.'

'You think he'll stop behind us?' Colin asked.

'Maybe.' Doyle sincerely hoped not.

'He won't. If he really is an FBI man, he'll be too smart to fall for that kind of trick. He'll just zoom on by as if he doesn't notice us, then pick us up later.'

Alex was too tense to play the boy's game. His lips set in a tight, grim line, he slowed the car even more, looked back and saw that the rented van was also slowing down. His heart beating too rapidly, he drove on to the burm, gravel crunching under the wide tyres, and came to a full stop.

'Well?' Colin asked, excited by this turn of events.

Alex tilted the rear-view mirror and watched the Automover pull off the highway and stop just a quarter of a mile behind them. 'Well, he's not an FBI man, then.'

'Hey, great!' the boy said, apparently delighted

by the unexpected turn the day had taken. 'What could he be?'

'I don't like to think about that,' Doyle said.

'I do.'

'Think quietly, then.'

He let off the brake and drove back on to the Interstate, accelerated smoothly into the traffic pattern. Two cars came between them and the van, providing an illusory sense of isolation and safety. However, within a very few minutes the Chevrolet passed the other vehicles and insinuated itself behind the Thunderbird once more.

What does he want? Doyle wondered.

It was almost as if the stranger behind the wheel of the van somehow knew of Alex Doyle's secret cowardice and was playing on it.

The land was now even flatter than it had been, like a gigantic gameboard, and the road was straighter and more mesmeric.

They had passed the exit ramp for Effingham; and now all the signs were warning far in advance of the connecting route for Decatur, and marking the tens of miles to St Louis.

Alex kept the Thunderbird moving five miles faster than the speed limit, sweeping around the slower traffic but staying mostly within the right-hand lane.

The van would not be shaken.

Ten miles after their first stop, he slowed down and pulled over to the burm again, watched as the Chevrolet followed suit. 'What the hell does he *want*?' Doyle asked.

'I've been thinking about that,' Colin said, frowning. 'But I just can't figure him.'

When Doyle took the car back on the road again, he said, 'We can make more speed than a van like that. Lots more. Let's leave him in our dust.'

'Just like in the movies,' Colin said, clapping his hands. 'Tromp it down all the way!'

Although he was not as pleased as Colin was about the prospect of a high-speed escape and pursuit, Doyle gradually pressed the accelerator pedal to the floor. He felt the big car tremble, shimmy, then steady down as it raced towards the performance peak which was being demanded of it. In spite of the Thunderbird's nearly airtight insulation, the road noises came to them now: a dull but building background roar underlying the rhythmic pounding of the engine and the shrill, protesting cry of the gusting wind which strained through the bar grill.

When the speedometer registered a hundred miles an hour, Alex looked in the mirror again. Incredibly, the Chevrolet was pacing them. It was the only other vehicle in sight which was using the left-hand lane.

The Thunderbird picked up speed: one-oh-five (with the road noise like a waterfall crashing down all around them), one-ten (and the wind screaming wildly now), one-fifteen (the shimmy back, the frame sighing and groaning), then the top of the gauge, beyond the last white numerals and still moving, still increasing speed . . .

The median posts flashed past in a single, faultless blur, a wall of grey steel. Beyond that wall, in the eastbound lanes, cars and trucks went past in the opposite direction as if they had been shot out of a cannon.

The van lost ground.

'We're really moving!' Colin cried, his voice a mixture of glee and outright horror.

'And he isn't keeping up!' Alex said.

The van dwindled, disappeared behind them.

The highway was deserted up ahead. Doyle did not take his foot from the accelerator.

Startling the drivers of the other cars which they passed, eliciting a symphony of angrily blaring horns, they rocketed across Illinois at top speed for another five minutes, putting miles between themselves and the stranger in the van. They were half exhilarated and half panicked, caught up in the excitement of the chase.

However, with the Chevrolet out of sight now, and the sense of being hotly pursued thus dimmed, Doyle was made aware of the risk that he was taking by maintaining such a terribly high speed even in this light traffic. If a tyre blew . . .

Above the shrieking wind and the manic music of the road rushing under them, Colin said, 'What about radar?'

If they were stopped for speeding, would any right-thinking highway patrolman believe that they were fleeing from a mysterious man in a rented Automover? Fleeing from a man they did not even know, had never met – had never really even seen? Fleeing from a man who had neither harmed nor threatened to harm them? Fleeing from a complete stranger whom Alex feared only because – well, only because he had always been afraid of that which he could not fully understand? No, that kind of story would look like a lie, a clumsy excuse. It was too fantastic and, at the

same time, far too shallow. It would only antago-
nise a cop.

Reluctantly Doyle eased back on the accelerator. The speedometer needle fell rapidly to the
one-hundred mark, quivered there like a hesitant
finger, then dropped even lower.

Doyle looked in the mirror.

The van was nowhere in sight. For a few
minutes, anyway, they would be unobserved by
the driver of the Chevrolet.

'He's probably coming up fast,' Colin said.

'Exactly.'

'What are we going to do?'

Immediately ahead was the exit for Route 51
and signs announcing the distance to Decatur.

'We'll use secondary roads for the rest of the
day,' Alex said. 'Let him hunt for us along Route
70 if he wants.'

He used the Thunderbird's brakes for the first
time in a long while, and drove down the exit
ramp into that flat country.

Six

From Decatur, they took the secondary Route 36 west to the end of the state, then followed it into Missouri. The land was even flatter than it had been during the morning; the fabled prairies were a monotonous spectacle. Just past noon, Alex and the boy ate a quick lunch at a trim white-clapboard café and then pressed on.

Not far beyond the turnoff for Jacksonville, Colin said, 'What do you think, then?'

'About what?'

'The man in the Chevrolet.'

The westering sun glared on the windscreen.

'What about him?' Doyle asked.

'Who could he be?'

'Isn't he FBI?'

'That was just a game.'

For the first time Alex realized how much the ubiquitous van had affected the boy, how much it had unsettled him. If Colin was no longer interested in his games, he must be quite disturbed, and he deserved a straightforward reply.

'Whoever he is,' Doyle said, shifting his aching buttocks on the vinyl seat, 'he's dangerous.'

'Somebody we know?'

'No. I think he's a complete stranger.'

'Then why is he after us?'

'Because he needs to be after *someone*.'

'That's no answer.'

Doyle thought about that special breed of madmen which had grown out of the previous decade, out of those pressure-cooker years when the very fabric of society had been heated to the boiling point and very nearly melted away. He thought about men like Charles Manson, Richard Speck, Charles Whitman, Arthur Bremer . . . Though Charles Whitman, the Texas tower sniper who had shot more than a dozen innocent people, might have been suffering from an undiagnosed brain tumour, the others had not required any physical illness or rational explanations for the bloodletting they had caused. The slaughter – which had been legitimized by a government which gloated over the 'body counts' from Vietnam – had been, in itself, the reason and explanation for the event. There were at least a dozen other names that Doyle could no longer recall, men who had murdered wantonly but not sufficiently to gain immortality. Since 1963 a madman had to be either clever in his methods, selective enough to choose the famous as his targets, or ruthless enough to cut down a dozen or more people before he was at all memorable. The videotape replay of an assassination and the nightly broadcasting of a bloody war had dulled American sensitivities. The single murderous impulse had become far too common to be at all noteworthy . . . Doyle attempted to convey these thoughts to Colin, couching them in grisly terms only when no other terms would do.

'You think he's crazy, then?' the boy asked when Doyle was finished.

'Perhaps. Actually, he hasn't done much of anything yet. But if we had stayed on the throughway and let him follow us, given him time and plenty of opportunity . . . Who knows what he might have done, eventually?'

'This all sounds para—'

'Paranoid?'

'That's the word,' Colin said, shaking his head approvingly. 'It sounds very paranoid.'

'These days you have to be somewhat paranoid,' Doyle said. 'It's almost a vital requirement for survival.'

'Do you think he'll find us again?'

'No.' Doyle blinked as the sun glimmered especially brightly against the windscreen. 'He'll stay on the Interstate, trying like hell to catch up with us again.'

'Sooner or later he's going to realize we got off.'

'But he won't know where or when,' Doyle said. 'And he can't know where, exactly, we'll be going.'

'What if he finds someone else to pick on?' Colin asked. 'If he just started to tail us because we happened to be going west on the same road he was using – won't he choose some other victim when he realizes that we've gotten away from him?'

'What if he does?' Doyle asked.

'Shouldn't we let the police know about him?' the boy asked.

'You've got to have proof before you can accuse anyone,' Doyle said. 'Even if we had proof, incontrovertible proof, that the man in the Chevrolet intended to hurt us, we couldn't do anything with it. We don't know *whom* to accuse, not by name. We don't know where he's headed, except westward. We don't have a number for the van, anything the cops could use to trace it.' He looked at Colin, then back at the blacktop road. 'All we can do is thank our stars we got rid of him.'

'I guess so.'

'You better believe it.'

Much later Colin said, 'When he was following us, pulling off the road behind us, speeding to catch up with us – were you scared?'

Doyle hesitated only a second, wondering if he should admit to some less unmanly reaction: uneasiness, disquiet, alarm, anxiety. But he knew that, with Colin, honesty was always best. 'Of course I was scared. Just a little bit, but scared nonetheless. There was reason to be.'

'I was scared too,' the boy said without embarrassment. 'But I always thought that when you got to be an adult, you didn't have to be scared of anything any more.'

'You'll outgrow some fears,' Doyle said. 'For instance . . . are you afraid of the dark at all?'

'Some.'

'Well, you will outgrow that. But you don't outgrow everything. And you find new things to be afraid of.'

They crossed the Mississippi River at Hannibal instead of St Louis, missing the Gateway Arch altogether. Just before the turnoff to Hiawatha, Kansas, they left Route 36 for a series of connecting highways that took them south once more to

Interstate 70 and, by eight-fifteen, to the Plains Motel near Lawrence, Kansas, where they had reservations for the night.

The Plains Motel was pretty much like the Lazy Time, except that it had only one long wing and was built of grey stone and clapboard instead of bricks. The signs were the same orange and green neon. The Coke machine by the office door might have been moved, during the day, from the Lazy Time near Indianapolis; the air around it was cool and filled with robotic noises.

Alex wondered if the desk clerk would be a stout woman with a beehive hair style.

Instead, it was a man Doyle's age. He was clean-shaven, his hair neatly trimmed. He had a square, honest, *American* face, perfect for recruitment posters. He could have made a fortune doing television commercials for Pepsi, Gillette, Schick, and full-page ads for Camel cigarettes in all the magazines.

'I noticed a no-vacancy sign outside,' Doyle said. 'I wondered if you'd held our room. We're an hour later than the reservations called for, but—'

'Is it Doyle?' the man asked, revealing perfect white teeth.

'Yes.'

'Sure, I held it.' He produced a flimsy form from the desk.

'Hey, good news! I know you must have been worried about getting stuck—'

'Wasn't worried at all, Mr Doyle. If you hadn't reserved it, I'd have had to rent it to coons.'

Doyle was weary from a long day on the road,

93

and he could not decide what the clerk meant. 'Coons?'

'Niggers,' the clerk said. 'Three times they came in. If I didn't have your reservation, I'd have had to let one of them take 22 for the night. And I hate that. I'd rather let a room stand empty all night than rent to one of them.'

Doyle felt as if he were giving his approval to the man's bigotry when he signed the registration paper. He wondered, briefly, why he, dressed and groomed as he was, made any better impression than the blacks who had stopped before him.

When the handsome young man gave Doyle the room key, he said, 'What kind of gas mileage you get on that T-Bird?'

Alex had known his share of bigots, and he was expecting this one, like the others, to continue with his practised invective. He was surprised, then, by the change of subject. 'Mileage? I don't know. I never checked.'

'I'm saving for a car like that. Gas hogs, but I love them. Car like that tells you about a man. You see a man in a T-Bird, you know he's making it.'

Alex looked at the room key in his hand. 'Twenty-two? Where's that?'

'To the right, clear at the end. Nice room, Mr Doyle.'

Alex went out to the car. He knew why the clerk accepted him. The Thunderbird was, for that man, a symbol which eclipsed reality. A car like that transformed a counter-culture freak into a mere eccentric, so far as the clerk was concerned. That attitude depressed Alex. He had not expected that here in the heartlands a man was defined by his possessions.

George Leland spent Tuesday night in a cheaper place three miles west of the Plains Motel. Though it was a tiny single room, he was not always alone. Courtney was often there. Sometimes he saw her standing in a corner, her back to the wall. Other times she sat on the foot of the bed or in the poorly padded plank chair by the bathroom door. He got angry with her more than once and told her to go away. She would vanish as quietly as she appeared. But then he would miss her and long for her – and she would return, making the cheaper place seem far more luxurious and grand than the Plains Motel.

He slept fitfully.

Two hours before dawn, unable to sleep at all any more, he got up and showered and dressed. He sat on the bed, several maps opened on the covers, and studied the route that would be followed Wednesday. He traced and retraced it with his blunt fingers.

Leland knew that somewhere in those six hundred miles he would have to take care of Doyle and the boy. He no longer needed to conceal this truth from himself. Courtney had helped him face up to it. He must kill them, just as he had killed that highway patrolman who tried to stand between him and Courtney. It was much too dangerous to put this thing off any longer. By tomorrow night they would be well over halfway to San Francisco. If Doyle decided to change their route for the last long leg of the journey, Leland might lose them for good.

Tomorrow, then. Somewhere between Lawrence, Kansas, and Denver. Leland would finally be striking back at Them, at everyone who had put him down and worked against him these last two years. This was the new beginning. From now on, he was not going to be pushed around. He would teach everyone to respect him. His luck would pick up, too. With Doyle and the kid out of the way, he and Courtney could go on together with their wonderful life. He would be all that she had, and she would cling to him.

A few minutes past six o'clock Tuesday evening, a call came through from the police lab. Detective Ernie Hoval took it in his sparsely furnished office on the second floor of the divisional headquarters building. 'This about the Pulham case?' he asked before the man on the other end of the line could say anything. 'If it's not, take it to someone else. I'm on the Pulham until it's solved, and nothing else.'

'You'll want this,' the lab man said. He sounded like the same balding, sallow, narrow man who had not been humbled by Detective Hoval the night before. 'We got the fingerprint report back from Washington. Just came in on the teletype.'

'And?'

'No record.'

Hoval hunched over his big desk, dwarfing it, the receiver clenched tightly in one hand, his other hand fisted on the blotter. His knuckles were white and sharp. 'No record?'

'I told you it might be that way,' the technician

said, almost as if he enjoyed Hoval's disappointment. 'I think this looks more like a nut case with every passing minute.'

'It's political,' Hoval insisted, his fist opening and closing again and again. 'Organized cop killing.'

'I don't agree.'

'You got proof otherwise?' Hoval asked angrily.

'No,' the technician admitted. 'We're still going over the car, but it looks hopeless. We've taken paint samples from every nick and scrape. But who knows if one of them was made by the killer's vehicle? And if one of them was – which one?'

'You sweep out the cruiser?' Hoval asked.

'Of course,' the technician said. 'We found a few hairs, pubic and otherwise. Nail clippings. Various kinds of mud. Blades of grass. Bits of food. Most of it has no connection with the killer. And even if some of it does – the hair, a couple of torn threads we picked off the door catch – we can't do much with it until we have a suspect to apply it to.'

'The case won't be solved with lab work,' Hoval agreed.

'What other leads you have?'

'We're reconstructing Pulham's shift,' Hoval said. 'Starting with the moment he took the squad car out of the garage.'

'Anything?'

'There are lots of minutes to account for, lots of people to talk with,' Hoval said. 'But we'll come up with something.'

'A nut,' the technician said.

'You're all wrong about that.' Hoval hung up.

Twenty years ago Ernie Hoval had become a cop because it was a profession and not just a job; it was work that brought a man a measure of honour and respect. It was hard work, the hours long, the pay only adequate, but it gave you the opportunity to contribute something to your community. The fringe benefits of police work – the gratitude of your neighbours and the respect of your own children – were more important than the salary. At least, that had been true in the past . . .

These days, Hoval thought, a cop was nothing more than a target. Everyone was after the police. Blacks, liberals, spics, peaceniks, women's liber-ationists – all the lunatic fringe revelled in making fools of the police. These days a cop was looked upon, at best, as a buffoon. At worst, he was called a fascist, and he was marked for death by these revolutionary groups that no one but other cops seemed to give a damn about . . .

It had all started in 1963, with Kennedy and Dallas. And it had gotten much, much worse through the war. Hoval knew that, although he could not understand why the assassinations and the war had so fundamentally changed so many people. There were other political murders in America's history, all without profound effect on the nation. And there had been other wars which had, if anything, strengthened our moral fibre. This war had had the opposite effect. He could not say why – except to point out that the communists and other revolutionary forces had long been looking for excuses to act – but he knew it to be true.

He thought about Pulham, latest victim of these changes, and he fisted both big hands. It *was* political. Sooner or later they *would* get the bastards.

Wednesday,
7:00 A.M.

—

Thursday,
7:00 A.M.

Seven

The morning held the threat of rain. Gently undulating fields of tender new wheat shoots touched the far horizons, a green carpet under the low grey ceiling of fast-moving clouds. Here and there on the maddeningly level land, enormous concrete grain elevators thrust up like gigantic lightning rods to test the mettle of the pending storm.

Colin liked it. He kept pointing to the grain elevators and to the occasional skeletal oil derricks which stood like prison watchtowers in the distance. 'It's great, isn't it?'

'This land's every bit as flat as that back in Indiana and Missouri,' Doyle said.

'But there's *history* here.' Today the boy was wearing a red-and-black Frankenstein T-shirt. It had pulled up out of his corduroy trousers, but he paid it no attention now.

'History?' Doyle asked.

'Haven't you heard of the Old Chisholm Trail? Or the Santa Fe Trail? All the famous Old West towns are here,' the boy said, excited about it. 'You have Abilene and Fort Riley, Fort Scott, Pawnee Rock, Wichita, Dodge City, and the old Boot Hill.'

'I didn't know you were a cowboy-movie fan,' Doyle said.

'I'm not, that much. But it's still exciting.'

Alex looked at the great plains and tried to picture them as they had once been: shifting sands, dust, cactus, a stark and foreboding landscape that had barely been touched by man. Yes, once it must have been a romantic place.

'There were Indian wars here,' Colin said. 'And John Brown caused a small civil war in Kansas back in 1856, when he and his boys killed five slave owners at Pottawatomie Creek.'

'Bet you can't say that five times, fast.'

'A dollar?' Colin asked.

'You're on.'

'Pottawatomie, Pottawatomie, Pottawatomie, Pottawatomie, Pottawatomie!' he said, breathless at the end of it. 'You owe me a buck.'

'Put it on my tab,' Doyle said. He felt loose and easy and good again, now that the trip was turning out to be what they had planned.

'You know who else came from Kansas?'

'Who?'

'Carry Nation,' Colin said, giggling. 'The woman who went around breaking up saloons with an axe.'

They passed another grain elevator sitting at the end of the long, straight, blacktop road.

'Where did you learn all this?' Doyle asked.

'Just picked it up,' Colin said. 'Bits and pieces from here and there.'

Now and then they passed fields which were standing idle, rich brown patches of land like neatly opened tablecloths. In one of these, a fifty-foot-high whirlwind gathered dust in a compact column of whining spring air.

'This is also where Dorothy lived,' Colin said, watching the whirlwind.

'Dorothy who?'

'The girl in *The Wizard of Oz*. Remember how she got carried to Oz by a tremendous tornado?'

Alex was about to answer when he was startled by the brash roar of an automobile horn immediately behind them. He looked at the mirror – and sucked air between his teeth when he saw the Chevrolet van. It was no more than six feet from their rear bumper. The unseen driver was pounding the palm of his hand into the horn ring: *beep, beep, beep, beep, beep, beeeeeep!*

Doyle looked at the speedometer, saw that they were doing better than seventy. If he had been so surprised by the horn that he had stomped the brake pedal, the Chevrolet would have run right over them. And they would all be dead.

'Stupid sonofabitch,' he said.

Beep, beeeeeeep, beeeeeep . . .

'Is it him?' Colin asked.

'Yes.'

The van moved up, so close now that Doyle could not even see its bumper or the bottom third of its grill.

'Why's he blowing his horn?' Colin asked.

'I don't know . . . I guess – to make sure we know he's back.'

Eight

The van's horn played a monotonous dirge.

'Do you think he wants you to stop?' Colin asked, gripping his knees in his delicate hands and leaning forward as if bent by the tension.

'I don't know.'

'Are you going to stop?'

'No.'

Colin nodded. 'Good. I don't think we should stop. I think we should keep going no matter what.'

Doyle expected that any second now the stranger would stop blowing his horn and let the van fall back to its customary quarter of a mile. Instead, it just hung in there, only three feet away from their back end now, cruising at seventy miles an hour, horn blaring.

Whether or not the man in the Chevy was as dangerous as a Charles Manson or Richard Speck, he was most certainly unbalanced. He was getting some sort of kick out of terrorising complete strangers, and that was far from normal. More than ever before, Doyle knew he did not want to confront this man face-to-face and test the limits of his madness.

Beep, beep, beeeeeep . . .

'What can we do?' the boy asked.

Doyle glanced at him. 'Seatbelt on?'

'Of course.'

'We'll outrun him again.'

'And go to Denver on the back roads?'

'Yeah.'

'He'll just pick us up again tomorrow morning when we leave Denver on the way to Salt Lake City.'

'No, he won't,' Doyle said.

'How can you be sure?'

'He's not clairvoyant,' Doyle said. 'He's just been lucky, that's all. By chance, he's stayed in the approximate area where we've stayed each night – and equally by chance, he's started out around the same hour each morning that we started out. It's purely coincidental, the way he keeps catching up to us.' He knew that this was the only rational explanation, as weak as it was, the only thing that made any sense. Yet he did not believe a word of it. 'You read about dozens of wilder coincidences in the newspapers. All the time.' He was talking, now, only to calm the boy. That old, familiar, dreaded fear of his had returned, and he knew that he would not be calm again, himself, until they were safely in San Francisco.

He pressed down on the accelerator.

The Thunderbird surged forward, opening a gap between them and the Chevrolet. The gap rapidly widened, even though the Automover put on its own burst of speed.

'You'll have a lot more driving to do if we go the back way,' the boy said, a vague apprehension in his voice.

'Not necessarily. We can go north and pick up Route 36 again,' Doyle said, watching the van dwindle in the rear-view mirror. 'That's a pretty good road up there.'

'It'll still mean an extra couple of hours. Yesterday you were really tired when we got to the motel.'

'I'll be all right,' Doyle said. 'Don't you worry about me.'

They took Connecting Route 77 north to Route 36 and went west across the top of the state.

Colin no longer found the fields, grain elevators, oil derricks, and dust storms especially interesting. He hardly looked at the scenery. He tucked in his Frankenstein T-shirt and smoothed it down, played tunes on his bony knees, cleaned his thick glasses, and smoothed his shirt some more. The minutes passed like snails.

Leland let the van slow down to seventy, quietening the furniture and household goods which rattled noisily in the cargo hold when he drove any faster. He looked at the golden, transparent girl beside him. 'They must have turned off somewhere along the way. We won't catch up with them until we get into Denver this evening.'

She said nothing.

'I should have stayed back a ways until I saw a chance to run them off the road. I shouldn't have pressured him like that right away.'

She only smiled.

'Well,' he said, 'I guess you're right. The highway's too public a place to take care of them. Tonight, at the motel, will be better. I might be able to do it with the knife, if I can sneak up on them. No noise that way. And they won't be expecting anything there.'

The fields flashed past. The leaden sky grew lower, and rain spattered across the windshield. The wipers thumped hypnotically, like a club slammed again and again into something soft and warm.

Nine

The Rockies Motor Hotel, on the eastern edge of Denver, was an enormous complex in the shape of a two-storey tick-tack-toe grid, with one hundred rooms in each of its four long wings. Despite its size – nearly two miles of concrete-floored, open-air, metal roofed corridors – the place seemed small, for it stood in the architectural shadow of the city's high-rise buildings and, more impressively, in view of the magnificent snow-capped Rocky Mountains which loomed up to the west and south. During the day the high country sun gleamed on the ranks of precisely duplicated windows and on the steel rain spouting, transformed the tops of the long walkway awnings into corrugated mirrors, shimmered on the Olympic swimming pool in the enclosed centre of the courtyard grid. At night warm orange lamps glowed behind the curtains in most of the rooms, and there were also lights in the pool and around the pool; and the front of the motel was a blaze of yellow, white, and red lights which were there chiefly to draw attention to the office, lobby, restaurant, and Big Rockies Cocktail Lounge.

At ten o'clock Wednesday night, however, the motel was dim and drab. Although all the usual lights were burning, they could not cast back the driving grey rain and the thin night mist which carried a reminder of the winter chill that had not been long gone from the city. The cold rain bounced on the macadam parking lot, thundered on the rows of cars, and pattered against the sheet-glass walls of the lobby and restaurant. It drummed insistently on the roofs and on the rippled awnings that covered the promenades on every wing, a pleasant sound which lulled most of the overnight guests into a quick, deep sleep. The rain chattered noisily into the swimming pool and puddled at the base of the spruce trees and other evergreens which dotted the well-landscaped grounds. It sloshed out of the rain spouting and swirled along kerb gutters, and made momentary lakes around drainage grills. The mist reached what the rain could not, beading on sheltered windows and on the slick red enamel of the numbered room doors.

In room 318, Alex Doyle sat on the edge of one of the twin beds and listened both to the rain on the roof and to Colin talking on the telephone to Courtney.

The boy did not mention the stranger in the rented van. The man had not caught up to them again during the long afternoon. And he had no way of knowing where they were spending the night . . . Even if this game had begun to intrigue him enough to send him out of his way in order to keep it going, he would be discouraged by the bad weather; he would not be searching at all the motels along the Interstate in hopes of locating the Thunderbird — not tonight, not in the rain.

There was no need to worry Courtney with the details of a danger which had passed and which, Doyle felt now, had-never been much of a danger to begin with.

Colin finished and handed the receiver to Doyle.

'How did *you* like Kansas?' she asked when he said hello.

'It was an education,' Doyle said.

'With Colin as your teacher.'

'That sums it up.'

'Alex, is anything wrong with him?'

'Colin?'

'Yes.'

'Nothing's wrong. Why do you ask?'

She hesitated. The open line hissed softly between them like a subdued echo of the cold rain thundering across the motel roof. 'Well . . . He's not as exuberant as usual.'

'Even Colin gets tired,' Doyle said, winking at the boy.

Colin nodded grimly. He knew what his sister was asking and what Alex was trying to avoid telling her. When he had spoken to her, Colin had tried to be natural. But his practised chatterboxiness had not been able to fully cover over the simmering fear he'd kept on the back burner since the van had appeared early this morning.

'That's all?' Courtney asked Doyle. 'He's just tired?'

'What else?'

'Well—'

'We're both road-weary,' Doyle interrupted. He knew that she sensed more to it than just that.

Sometimes she was positively psychic. 'It's true that there's a lot to see on a cross-country drive – but most of it is exactly what you saw ten minutes ago, and ten minutes before *that*.' He changed the subject before she could press for more details. 'Any furniture arrive yet?'

'Oh yes!' she said. 'The bedroom suite.'

'And?'

'Just like it looked in the showroom. And the mattress is firm but full of bounce.'

He assumed a mock suspicious tone. 'How would you know about that – what with your husband halfway across the country?'

'I jumped up and down on it for about five minutes,' she said, chuckling quietly. 'Testing it, you know?'

He laughed, picturing the slim, long-haired, elfin-faced girl romping happily on their bed as if it were a trampoline.

'And you know what, Alex?'

'What?'

'I was nude when I tested it. How's that strike you?'

He stopped laughing. 'Strikes me fine.' His voice caught in the back of his throat. He felt himself smile idiotically, even though Colin was watching and listening. 'Why torture me like this?'

'Well, I keep thinking you might meet some saucy woman on the highway and run off with her. I don't want you to forget me.'

'I couldn't,' he said, speaking beyond sex now. 'I couldn't forget.'

'Well, I like to be sure. And – hey, I think I found a job.'

'Already?'

'There's a new city magazine starting up, and they need a photographer to work full time. No tedious layout jobs. Just straight photography. I made an appointment to show them my portfolio tomorrow.'

'Sounds great.'

'It'll be good for Colin, too,' she said. 'It's not an office job. I'll be running all over the city, setting up shots. That ought to make a pretty full summer for him.'

They talked only a few minutes more, then said their goodbyes. When he hung up the phone, the drumming rain seemed to get suddenly louder.

Later, in the intensely dark room, as they lay in their beds waiting for sleep to come, Colin sighed and said, 'Well, she knew that something was wrong, didn't she?'

'Yes.'

'You can't fool Courtney.'

'Not for very long, anyway,' Doyle said, staring at the lightless ceiling and thinking about his wife.

The darkness seemed to swell and shrink and swell again, to pulse as if it were alive, to press warmly down around them like a blanket.

'You really think we've lost him?' the boy asked.

'Sure.'

'We thought we'd lost him before.'

'This time we can be certain.'

'I hope you're right,' Colin said. 'He's a real crazy, whoever he is.'

The shushing snare-drum music of the spring

storm soon put the boy, and then Doyle, to sleep . . .

Rain was falling as steadily as ever when Colin woke him. He stood beside Doyle's bed, shaking the man by the shoulder and whispering urgently. *'Alex! Alex, wake up. Alex!'*

Doyle sat up in bed, groggy and somewhat confused. His mouth felt furry and stale. He kept blinking his eyes, trying to see something, until he realized it was the middle of the night and the room was still pitch-black.

'Alex, are you awake?'

'Yeah. What's the matter?'

'There's someone at the door,' the boy said.

Alex stared straight at the door but could see nothing of the boy. 'At the door?' he asked stupidly, still not clear-headed enough to understand what was happening.

'He woke me up,' Colin whispered. 'I've been listening to him maybe three or four minutes. I think he's trying to pick the lock.'

Ten

Now, above the background noise of the rain, Alex could hear the strange fumbling noises on the other side of the door. In the warm, close, anonymous darkness, the sounds of the wire probing back and forth in the lock seemed much louder than they really were. His fear acted as an amplifier.

'You hear him?' Colin asked. His voice cracked between the last two words, leaping up the scale.

Doyle reached out and found the boy and put one hand on his skinny shoulder. 'I can hear him, Colin,' he whispered, hoping his own voice would remain steady. 'It's okay. Nobody's going to come in here. Nobody's going to hurt you.'

'But it must be *him*.'

Doyle looked at his wristwatch, which was the only source of light in the small room. The irradiated numerals jumped up at him, sharp and clear: seven minutes after three in the morning. At this hour no one had a legitimate reason for picking a lock on a room that . . . What was he thinking? There was no legitimate reason for such a thing at *any* hour, day or night.

'Alex, what if he gets in here?'

'Ssshh,' Doyle said, kicking back the covers and sliding out of bed.

'What if he *does*?'

'He won't.'

Doyle went to the door, aware that Colin was right behind him, and he bent down to listen at the lock. Metal rasped on metal, clinked, snicked, rasped again.

He stepped sideways to the room's only window, just to the left of the door. Careful not to make a sound, he lifted the heavily lined drapes and then the cold venetian blinds. He tried to look to the right along the covered promenade where the man would be bent over the lock, but he found that the outside of the glass was sheathed in a fine white mist which made the window completely opaque. He could not see anything through it except the vague, diffused glow of several scattered motel lights that made the darkness beyond somewhat less intense and more manageable than that within the room.

With as much care as he had employed in raising them away from the window, he dropped the blinds and the drapes back into place. He could not see any good reason for continued silence, but he took the precaution anyway, in order to waste a few more precious seconds . . . Any moment, he knew, the time would come for him to make a decision, to chart some response to this – yet he did not know for sure if he was capable of acting against whoever was out there.

He went back to the door.

The carpet was nubbed and prickly against his bare feet.

Colin had remained by the door, silent, invisible in the onyx shadows, perhaps too frightened to move or speak.

The icy sound of the wire scraping inside the lock was insistent and as loud as ever. It made Alex think of the surgeon's scalpel worrying at the hard surface of a bone.

'Who's there?' Doyle finally asked. He was surprised at the strength and self-possession so evident in his voice. Indeed, he was surprised that he could even speak at all.

The wire stopped moving.

'Who's there?' Doyle demanded once more, louder this time, but with less genuine courage and more false bravado than before.

Rapid footsteps – certainly those of a large man – sounded on the concrete promenade floor and were quickly swallowed up in the steady roar of the storm.

They waited, listening intently. But the man was gone.

Alex fumbled for the light switch by the door, found it.

For a moment they were both blinded by the sudden glare. Then the familiar lines of the tritely designed motel room filtered back to them.

'He'll return,' Colin said.

The boy was standing by the desk, wearing only his skivvies and his Coke-bottle glasses. His thin brown legs were trembling uncontrollably, the bony knees nearly knocking together. Doyle, also standing there in his underwear, wondered if his own body was betraying his state of mind.

'Maybe not,' he said. 'Now that he knows we're up and around, he might not risk coming back.'

Colin was adamant. 'He will.'

Doyle knew what the situation demanded, but he did not want to face up to it. He did not want to go out there in the rain, looking for the man who had tried to pick the room lock.

'We could call the police,' Colin said.

'Oh? We still haven't anything to tell them, any proof. We'd sound like a couple of raving lunatics.'

Colin went back to his bed and sat down, pulled the blanket around himself, so that he looked like a miniature American Indian.

In the bathroom, Doyle drew a glass of tap water and drank it slowly, swallowing with some difficulty.

As he rinsed the glass and put it on the fake-marble shelf beside the porcelain sink, he caught sight of his face in the mirror. He was pale and haggard. The fear was etched in painfully obvious lines at the corners of his bloodless mouth and all around his eyes. He did not like what he saw, and he could barely meet his own gaze.

Christ, he thought, doesn't the frightened little boy ever fade away and let the man come through? Won't you ever outgrow it, Alex? Are you going to be so easily terrified all the rest of your life? Now that you have a wife to protect? Do you think that maybe Colin will grow up fast enough so that he will be able to look after both you and Courtney?

Angry with himself, half ashamed, but still undeniably frightened, he turned away from the mirror and his own accusing countenance, and went back into the main room.

Colin had not moved from the bed or dropped the blanket from his shoulders. He looked at Doyle, his large eyes magnified by the eyeglasses, the speck of fear magnified as well. 'What would he have done if he'd been able to pick the lock without waking us?'

Doyle stood there in the middle of the room, unable to answer.

'When he got in here with us,' the boy said, 'what would he have done? Like you said when all this started – we don't have anything worth stealing.'

Doyle nodded stupidly.

'I think he's just what you said,' Colin went on. 'I think he's like one of those people you read about in the papers. I think he's a maniac.' His voice had become almost inaudible.

Though he knew that it was no real answer and was probably even untrue, Alex said, 'Well . . . he's gone now.'

Colin just looked at him.

The boy's expression might have meant anything, or nothing at all. But Alex saw in it the beginnings of doubt and a subtle shift of judgment. The boy, he felt certain, was re-evaluating him just as surely as the rain pattered on the roof overhead. And although Colin was far too intelligent to sum up anyone in an absolute term or category, too clever to think in blacks and whites, his opinion of Doyle was this minute changing for the worse, no matter how minimally.

But, Doyle asked himself, did one child's

opinion mean all that much to him? And he knew
immediately that when it was this child, the
answer was yes. All of his life Doyle had been
afraid of people, too timid to let himself be close
to anyone. He had been too unsure of himself to
risk loving. Until he had met Courtney. And
Colin. And now their opinions of him were more
important than anything else in the world.

He heard his own voice as if it had come from
someone else. 'I guess I better go outside and have
a look around. If I can get a glimpse of him, see
what he looks like, get the license number for that
van of his . . . Then we'll at least know something
about our enemy. He won't be such a cipher – and
he'll seem less frightening.'

'And if he does try anything serious,' Colin
said, 'we'll have a description to give the cops.'

Doyle nodded numbly, then went to the closet
and took out the rumpled, soiled clothes he had
worn the day before. He got dressed.

At the door a few minutes later, he looked
back at Colin. 'Will you be all right here by yourself?'

The boy nodded and drew the blanket tightly
around himself.

'I'll lock the door when I go out – and I won't
take a key. Don't open up for anyone but me. And
don't even open for me until you're certain that
you recognize my voice.'

'Okay.'

'I won't be long.'

Colin nodded again. Then, as frightened as he
was for himself and for Alex, he managed a bit of
gallows humour. 'You better be careful. It would

be utterly tasteless for an artist to let himself be killed in a cheap, dismal place like this.'

Doyle smiled grimly. 'No chance.' Then he went outside, making sure the door had locked behind him.

Earlier in the evening and fifteen hundred miles to the east, Detective Ernie Hoval opened the front door of a thirty-thousand-dollar three-bedroom ranch house in a pleasant middle-class development between Cambridge and Cadiz, Ohio, just off Route 22, and stepped into an entrance foyer which was liberally splashed with blood. Long red stains smeared the walls on both sides where desperate hands had slid down the plaster. Thick droplets of blood spotted the beige carpet and the yellow-brocade loveseat by the coat closet.

Hoval closed the door and walked into the living room, where a dead woman lay half on the sofa and half on the floor. She had been in her late forties, rather handsome if not pretty, tall and dark. She had taken a shotgun blast in the stomach.

Newspaper reporters and lab photographers circled her like wolves. Four lab technicians, as silent as a quartet of deaf-mutes, crawled all over the big room on their hands and knees, measuring and charting the spray patterns of the blood, which seemed to have reached into every nook and cranny. They were more likely fighting to keep from being sick.

'Christ,' Hoval said.

He went through the living room and down the narrow hall to the first bathroom, where there was an extremely pretty teenage girl sprawled at the foot of a bloodstained commode. She was wearing skimpy blue panties, nothing else, and had been shot once in the back of the head. The bathroom was even bloodier than the foyer and the living room combined.

In the smallest bedroom, a good-looking, long-haired, bearded boy in his early twenties was lying on his back in bed, covers drawn up to his chin, his hands folded peacefully on his chest. The pastel blanket was soaked with blood and shredded in the centre by shotgun pellets. The poster of the Rolling Stones stapled to the wall above the bed was streaked with red and curled damply at the edges.

'I thought you were only working on the Pulham case.'

Hoval turned to see who had spoken and confronted the ineffectual-looking lab man who had lifted the killer's fingerprints from Rich Pulham's squad car. 'I heard the report of the initial find and thought maybe this was tied in. It is kind of similar.'

'It was a family thing,' the lab man said.

'They already have a suspect?'

'They already have a *confession*,' the technician said, glancing uninterestedly at the dead boy on the bed.

'Who?'

'Husband and father.'

'He killed his own family?' This was not the first time Hoval had encountered a thing like that, but it never failed to shock him. His own wife and kids meant too much to him, were too intricate a part of his life for him to ever understand how another man could bring himself to slaughter his own flesh and blood.

'He was waiting for the arresting officers,' the technician said. 'He was the one who telephoned for them.'

Hoval felt ill.

'Anything on the Pulham situation?'

Hoval leaned against the wall, remembered the blood, pulled away and checked for stains. But the wall here was clean. He leaned back again, uneasy, a chill coursing along his spine. 'We think we have something,' he told the technician. 'It might have started at Breen's Café back at the interchange.' He summarized what they had learned from Janet Kinder, the waitress who had served an unnamed oddball his lunch Monday afternoon. 'If Pulham went after the man – and it looks more and more like he did – then our killer is driving a rented van on his way to California.'

'Hardly enough data for you to put out an APB, is there?'

Hoval nodded glumly. 'Must be a thousand Automovers going west on I-70. It'll take weeks to go through them all, trace the drivers, winnow it down to the bastard that did it.'

'This waitress give a description?' the lab man asked.

'Yeah. She's man-crazy, so she remembers these things well.' He repeated the description they had got from the waitress.

'He doesn't sound like a left-wing revolutionary to me,' the lab man said. 'More like an ex-marine.'

'There's no way to tell these days,' Ernie Hoval said. 'The SDS and some of these other crazies are cutting their hair, shaving, bathing, blending right in with your decent average citizens.' He was impatient with the sallow man and did not want to pursue the subject; quite obviously they were not on the same wavelength. He leaned away from the wall and looked once more into the bloody bedroom. 'Why?'

'Why this? Why'd he kill his own family?'

'Yes.'

'He's very religious,' the technician said, smiling again.

Hoval didn't get it. He said so.

'He's a lay preacher. Very dedicated to Christ, you know. Spreads the Good Word as much as he can, reads the Bible for an hour every night . . . Then he sees his boy going off the deep end with drugs – or at least with pot. He thinks his daughter's got loose morals or maybe no morals at all, because she won't tell him who she's dating or why she stays out so late. And the mother took up for both the kids a little too much. She was encouraging them to sin, as it were.'

'And what finally set him off?' Hoval asked.

'Nothing much. He says that all the little day-to-day things mounted up until he couldn't stand it any longer.'

'And the solution was murder.'

'For him, anyway.'

Hoval shook his head sadly, thinking of the pretty girl lying on the bathroom floor. 'What's the world coming to these days?'

'Not the world,' the slim man said. 'Not the *whole* world.'

Eleven

It was a hard rain, a downpour, a seemingly perpetual cloudburst. The wind from the east pushed it across high Denver in vicious, eroding sheets. It streamed off the peaked black-slate roofs of the four motel wings, chuckled rather pleasantly along the horizontal sections of spouting, roared down the wide vertical spouts, and gushed noisily into the drainage gratings in the ground. Everywhere, trees dripped, shrubs dripped, and flat surfaces glistened darkly. Dirty water collected in depressions in the courtyard lawn. The hard-driven droplets shattered the crystalline tranquillity of the swimming pool, danced on the flagstones laid around the pool, flattened the tough grass that encircled the flagstones.

The gusting wind brought the rain under the awning and into the second-level promenade outside of Doyle's room. The moment he closed the door, locking Colin inside, a whirlwind of cold water raced along the walkway and spun over him, soaking his right side. His blue work shirt and one leg of his well-worn jeans clung uncomfortably to his skin.

Shivering, he looked southward, down the longest stretch of the walkway, to the courtyard steps at the far end. The shadows were deep. None of the rooms had light in them; and the weak night lights on the promenade were spaced fifty or sixty feet apart. The night mist complicated the picture, curling around the iron awning supports and eddying in the recessed entrances to the rooms. Nevertheless, Doyle was fairly sure that there was no one prowling about in that direction.

Thirty feet to the north, two rooms beyond their own, another wing of the motel grid intersected this one, forming the northeast corner of the courtyard overlook. Whoever had been at their door might have run up there in a second, might have ducked quickly out of sight . . . Alex tucked his head down to keep the rain out of his face, hurried up that way and peered cautiously around the corner.

There was nothing down the short arm of that corridor except more red doors, the night mist, darkness, and wet concrete. A blue safety bulb burning behind a protective wire cage marked another set of open steps that led down to the first level, this time to the parking lot which completely ringed the complex.

The last segment of his own walkway, running off to the north, was equally deserted, as was the remainder of the second-level east-west wing.

He walked back to the wrought-iron railing and looked down into the courtyard at the pool and the landscaped ground around it. The only things that moved down there were those stirred by the wind and the rain.

Suddenly Alex had the eerie notion that he was

not merely alone out here – but that he was the only living soul in the entire motel. He felt as if all the rooms were empty, the lobby empty, the manager's quarters empty, all of it abandoned in the wake – or perhaps the approach – of some great cataclysm. The overbearing silence, except for the rain, and the bleak concrete hallways generated and fed this odd fantasy until it became disturbingly real and a bit upsetting.

Don't let the frightened little kid come to the surface again, Doyle warned himself. You've done well so far. Don't lose your cool now.

After a few minutes of observation, during which he leaned with both hands on the fancy iron safety railing, Doyle was convinced that the miniature pine trees and the neatly trimmed shrubbery in the courtyard below did not conceal anyone; their shadows were entirely their own.

The crisscrossing promenades remained quiet, deserted.

The windows were all dark.

Underneath the steadily drumming rain and the occasional banshee cries of the storm wind, the sepulchral silence continued undisturbed.

Standing by the rail, Alex had been without protection, and now he was thoroughly drenched. His shirt and trousers were sodden. Water had even gotten into his boots and had made his socks all cold and squishy. His arms were decorated with rank on rank of goose pimples, and he was shivering uncontrollably. His nose was running, and his eyes were teary from squinting out at the rain and fog.

Nevertheless, Doyle felt better than he had for

some time. Although he had not found the stranger who was harassing them, he had at least *tried* to confront the man. Finally, he had done something more than run away from the situation. He could have remained in the room despite Colin's accusing look, could have made it through the night without taking this risk. But he *had* taken the risk, after all, and now he felt somewhat better, pleased with himself.

Of course, there was nothing more to be done. Whoever the stranger was, and whatever the hell he had intended to do once he had picked their lock, the man had obviously lost interest in his game when he realized that they were awake and onto him. He would not be back tonight. Perhaps they would never see him again at all, here or anywhere.

When he turned and started back towards their room, all of his good humour was abruptly forgotten . . .

Two hundred feet along the same walkway which he had first examined on coming out of the room, along a corridor that had appeared to be absolutely empty and safe, a man stepped out of a recess in front of a door and hurried to the courtyard steps in the southeast corner of the overlook, thumped down them two at a time. He was very nearly invisible, thanks to the mist and the rain and the darkness. Doyle saw him only as a shapeless figure, a shadowy phantom . . . However, the hollow sound of his footsteps on the open stairs was proof that he was no imagined spirit.

Doyle went to the railing and looked down.

A big man dressed in dark clothes, made otherwise featureless by the night and the storm, loped across the lawn and the flagstones by the pool. He ducked under the floor of the second-level walkway which served as the roof over the first-level promenade.

Before he quite realized what he was doing, Alex started after the man. He ran to the head of the courtyard steps and went down fast, came out on the lawn where the rain and wind roiled openly.

The stranger was no longer over there on the ground-floor walkway where he had been when Doyle had last seen him. Indeed, he seemed to have vanished into thin air.

Doyle looked at the pines and shrubs from this new perspective, and he realized that the stranger might have doubled back to wait for him. The feathery shadows were menacing, far too deep and too dangerous . . .

Taking advantage of the yellow and green lights that surrounded the swimming pool and avoiding the shadows, Doyle crossed the courtyard without incident. However, he had no sooner gotten out of the worst of the wind and rain than he heard footsteps again. This time they were at the back of the complex, to the north, going up to the second level on this wing. He followed the hauntingly hollow *thump-thump-thump* which was barely audible above the rain sounds.

The stairwell was deserted when he got to it, a straight flight of wet and mottled grey-brown risers.

He stood at the bottom for a minute, looking up,

thinking. He was quite aware of the easy target that he would make when he came out at the top, all too vulnerable to a gun or knife or even to a quick shove that would carry him back down the way he had come.

Nevertheless, he started up, more than a little bit exhilarated and surprised at his own daring in having come even this far. Tonight he had begun to discover a new Alex Doyle inside the old one. There was a Doyle who could overcome the cowardliness when faced with a responsibility for the wellbeing of those he loved, when more than his own pride was affected.

He was not set upon when he came off the last step and into the northwest corner of the courtyard overlook. There was no one waiting for him. He was greeted by lightless windows, concrete, and red doors.

Again he experienced the strange feeling that he was the last man alive in the motel — indeed, that he was the last man in the world. He did not know if the fantasy was based on megalomania or paranoia, but the sense of isolation was complete.

Then Alex saw the stranger again. Shapeless, shadow-swathed, mist-draped, the man stood at the extreme north end of the promenade, at the head of the stairs which went down to the parking lot behind the motel complex. Another blue safety bulb behind another wire cage did nothing to illuminate the phantom. He took the first step, seemed to turn and look back at Doyle, took the second step, then the third, disappeared once more.

It's almost as if he *wants* me to follow him, Alex thought.

He went north along the promenade and down the rain-washed steps.

Twelve

Four mercury-vapour arc lamps towered over the parking area behind the Rockies Motor Hotel, making the night above them twice as dark as it was elsewhere, but somewhat illuminating the rows of cars beneath. The irritating, fuzzy purple light glinted dully in the falling raindrops and in the water that flushed across the black macadam. It made stark shadows. It leeched the colour out of everything it touched, transforming the once-bright cars into depressing, green-brown look-alikes.

Doyle, tinted a light purple himself, stood on the walk at the bottom of the stairwell and looked left and right along the lot.

The stranger was nowhere in sight.

Of course, the man might be hidden between two of the cars, crouched expectantly . . . But if the chase were to degenerate into a game of hide-and-seek in a playground of two or three hundred automobiles, they could waste all night darting around the silent machines and in and out of the shadows between them.

He supposed he had come to the end of it now; there was nothing to be gained by this expedition, after all. He was not going to get a look at the man

137

or at the rented Automover. He would have no description or licence number to work with or to give to the police – if it came to that. Therefore, he might as well go back to the room, get out of these wet clothes, towel off, and . . .

But he could not walk away from the challenge quite as easily as that. If he were not exactly drunk with courage, he was at least somewhat inebriated with his own appreciation for his new-found bravery. This brand-new Alex Doyle, this suddenly responsible Doyle, this Doyle who was capable of coping with and perhaps even over-coming his long-held fear, fascinated and pleased him immensely. He wanted to see just how far this previously unknown, even unsuspected, but certainly welcome strength would carry him, how deep this vein which he had tapped.

He went looking for the stranger.

The vending-machine room at the back of the motel complex did not have any doors on its two entrances. Cold white light fanned out in twin semicircles from both narrow archways, dispelling the sickly purple glow of the mercury-vapour lamps overhead.

Doyle went to the doorway and peered inside.

The room was well lighted and appeared untenanted. However, there were a number of blind spots formed by the bulky machines, a dozen places where a man could hide.

He stepped across the raised threshold.

The room was about twenty feet by ten feet. It contained twelve machines, which stood against the two longest walls and faced one another like teams of futuristic heavyweight prize fighters waiting for the bell to ring and the match to begin: three humming soda machines that could dispense six different flavours of bottled and canned refreshment; two squat cigarette machines; one cracker and cookie vender full of stale and half-stale goods; two sweet machines with an especially twenty-first-century look about them; a coffee and hot chocolate dispenser with stylised cups of steaming brown liquid painted on the mirrored front along with the bold legend **Sugar Cream Marshmallow**; a vender of peanuts, potato chips, pretzels, and cheese popcorn; and an ice machine which rattled noisily, continually, spitting newly made cubes into a shiny steel storage bin.

He walked slowly down the room, flanked by the murmuring dispensers, looking into the niche between each pair of them, expecting someone to jump out at him any second now. His tension and fear were qualitatively different from what he had known in the past; they were almost beneficial, clean, purgative. He felt a great deal like a small boy prowling through a most forbidding, decaying graveyard on Halloween night, a rag bag of conflicting emotions.

But the stranger was not in the room.

Doyle went outside again into the wind and rain, no longer much concerned with the bad weather, a man caught up in his own changes.

He walked along the parked cars, hoping to find the stranger kneeling between two of them. But he crossed from the end of one north-south wing to the end of the other north-south wing without noticing any movement or unlikely shadows.

He was just about to call it quits when he saw the weak light spilling out of the half-opened maintenance-room door. He had passed this way less than five minutes ago when he had been on his way to the vending machines, and this door had not been open then. And it was hardly an hour when the motel janitor would be coming to work . . .

Alex put his back to the wet concrete wall, his head resting in the centre of the neatly stencilled black-and-white sign which was painted there (MAINTENANCE AND SUPPLIES – MOTEL EMPLOYEES ONLY), and listened for movement inside the room.

A minute passed in silence.

Cautiously he reached out and pushed the oversized metal door all the way open. It swung inward without a sound, and an equally sound-less grey light came out.

Doyle looked inside. Directly across the large room, a second door, also metal and also over-sized, stood wide open to the rain. Beyond it was a section of the amoeboid parking lot. Good enough. The stranger had been here and had already gone.

He went into the room and looked around. It was slightly larger than the place that contained the vending machines. Towards the back, along the wall, were barrels of industrial cleaning compounds: soaps, abrasives, waxes, furniture polish. There were also electric floor waxers and buffers, a forest of long-handled mops and brooms and window-washing sponges. Two rid-ing lawn mowers stood in the middle of the room with a host of gardening tools and huge coils of transparent green plastic hose. At the front, closer to the doors, were the workbenches, carpentry tools, a standing jigsaw, and even a small wood lathe. To Doyle's right, the entire wall was covered with pegboard; the silhouettes of dozens of tools had been painted on the pegboard and the tools themselves hung over their own black outlines. The gardening axe was missing, but everything else was clean and hung neatly in place.

The barrels of cleaning compounds were too widely spaced and too small to effectively conceal a man, especially a man as tall and broadshouldered as the one whom he had seen crossing the courtyard earlier in the night.

Doyle walked further into the room and was halfway to the second door, only fifteen feet from it, when he suddenly understood the full implications of the missing axe on the pegboard. He almost froze in place. Then, warned by some sixth sense, he crouched and turned with more speed and agility than he had ever shown in his life.

Looming immediately behind him, nightmarishly large, the wild-eyed blond man raised both hands and swung the gardening axe.

Thirteen

Not once in his entire thirty years had Alex Doyle been in a fight – not a fist fight, wrestling match, or even a juvenile push-and-shove. He had never dealt out physical punishment to anyone, and neither had he taken any himself. Whether coward or genuinely committed pacifist or both, he had always managed to avoid controversial subjects in casual discussions, had avoided arguments and taking sides and forming relationships which might conceivably have led to violence. He was a civilized man. His few friends and acquaintances had always been as gentle as he was himself, and often even gentler. He was singularly unprepared to handle a raging maniac who was wielding a well-sharpened gardener's axe.

However, instinct served where experience failed. Almost as if he had been combat-trained, Alex fell backward, away from the glittering blade, and rolled across the grease-stained cement floor until he came up hard against the two riding lawn mowers.

His intellectual acceptance of the situation lagged far behind his automatic physical-emotional realization of the danger. He had heard the axe whistle past, inches from his head, and he knew what it would have done to him if it had found its mark . . . Yet, it was inconceivable that anyone could want to take his life, especially in such a sudden bloody fashion. He was Alex Doyle. The man without enemies. The man who had walked softly and carried no stick at all – the man who had often sacrificed his pride to save himself from just this sort of madness.

The stranger moved fast.

Dazed as he was, numb with surprise at the suddenness and extreme ferocity of the attack, Alex still saw the man coming.

The stranger lifted the axe.

'Don't!' Doyle said. He barely recognized his own voice. He had not lost all of his new-found courage. However, it was now tempered by a healthy fear which put it in the proper perspective.

The five-inch razored blade swept up, reached the top of its arc in one smooth movement, almost a precision instrument in those strong hands. Sharp slivers of light danced brightly on the cutting edge. The blade hesitated up there, high and cold and fantastic – and then it fell.

Alex rolled.

The axe dropped in his wake. It made the moist air whistle once again, and it thudded into a solid rubber tyre on one of the lawn mowers, splitting the deep tread.

Doyle came to his feet, and once more powered by a mindless drive for self-preservation, vaulted over one of the workbenches, clearing the four-foot width with more ease than he would ever have thought possible. He stumbled, though, and nearly fell flat on his face when he came down on the other side.

Behind him, the madman cursed: a curiously wordless, low grunt of anger and frustration.

Doyle turned, fully expecting the axe to cleave either his head or the surface of the wooden bench behind him. He had, at last, come to terms with his predicament. He knew that he might die here.

Across the room, the stranger hunched his broad shoulders and put all his strength into them, wrenched the blade free of the solid, uninflated tyre in which it had become wedged. He turned, his wet shoes scraping unpleasantly on the concrete floor, and he clutched the axe in both hands as if it were some sacred and all-powerful talisman which would ward off evil magic and protect the bearer from the work of malevolent sorcerers. There *was* something of the superstitious savage in this man, especially in and around those enormous dark-ringed eyes . . .

Those same eyes now located Doyle. Incredibly, the stranger bobbed his head and smiled.

Alex did not return the smile.

He *could not* return it. He was almost physically ill with premonitions of death, and he wished that he had never left the room.

He was still too far away from the doors to make a run for either of them. Before he could have crossed the open floor and gained the threshold, he would almost certainly have felt the axe blade bite down between his shoulder blades . . .

Rain dripping from his clothes, the stranger

moved in on Doyle, quiet and swift for such a large man. The noises which he had made outside, on the steps and promenades, could not have been accidental. He had been luring Alex along those shadowy corridors, drawing him to a place where he might be trapped.

A place like this.

Now only the wooden bench separated them.

'Who are you?' Doyle asked.

The stranger was no longer smiling when he stopped on the other side of the waist-high bench. In fact, he was frowning intensely, even wincing, as if he were being cruelly punched or jabbed with pins. What was it, what was on his mind? More than murder, now? He was annoyed considerably by *something*; that much was obvious. His mouth was set in a tight, straight, grim line, and he appeared to be struggling desperately to choke back a reaction to an inner pain.

'What do you want from us?' Doyle asked.

The man only glared at him.

'We've never hurt you.'

No answer.

'You don't even know us, do you?'

Even though his voice was weak, an involuntary whisper, and even though the terror that it betrayed might have goaded the madman into even bolder action, Doyle had to ask the questions. All of his life he had been able to settle other people's anger with sympathetic words, and now it became essential that he elicit some response – at least contrition – from this man. 'What have you to gain by hurting me?'

The madman swung the axe horizontally this

time, from right to left, trying to chop Doyle's torso from his legs.

It was close. His long arms had sufficient reach and strength to make the trick work, even with the bench between them. But Doyle saw it coming just in time to avoid it. He scrambled backward, out of the murderous arc.

Then he tripped over a large metal toolbox which he had not noticed. He windmilled his arms in a hopeless attempt to recover, lost his balance altogether. The room tilted around him. In that instant Doyle knew that he probably did not have a chance of getting out of this place alive. He was not going to return to Room 318, where Colin waited for him, was never going to finish the drive to San Francisco to see the new furniture in the new house or begin his wonderful new job with the agency or make love to Courtney again. Never. Falling, he saw the tall blond man start around the end of the workbench.

He did not stay down on the floor any measurable length of time, not even a second. The moment he hit, he pushed to his feet and staggered backward, trying to keep out of the madman's reach for at least one more precious minute.

In three short steps, however, he backed straight into the pegboard wall where the tools were hung.

Even as Doyle realized that he had nowhere left to run, the stranger stepped in front of him and swung the axe from right to left.

Doyle crouched.

The blade skimmed the pegboard above his head.

Rising even as he heard the axe whine by him, Doyle grabbed a heavy claw hammer which dangled from a hook on the wall. He had it in his hand when he was knocked sideways and down by a blow from the axe.

The hammer clattered across the floor.

But losing the hammer, Doyle thought, was the least of his troubles. The oppressive, pulsing pain in his side and chest made him all but helpless. Had he been cut up? Torn open? The pain . . . pain was terrible, the worst he had ever endured. But please, God, no . . . Please, please, not this. Not death. Not all the blood and having to lie in all the blood while the axe rose and fell and methodically dismembered him, not death, dammit. Anything else. All he could see on the other side of death was nothingness, perpetual blackness; and the vision was so complete and vivid and horrifying that he never even recognized the incongruity and futility of praying to a God in whose existence he did not believe. Just: God, God, please . . . Not this. Anything but this. Please . . .

All of this flashed through his mind in a fraction of a second, before he realized that he had not been caught by the axe blade. Instead, he had been hit on the backswing of the first blow. He had taken the *head* of the axe, the three-inch-wide top of it, just below the ribs on his right side. There had been enough force in the blow to knock the wind out of him and to leave him with a welt and eventually a bruise. But that was all. There was no torn flesh. No blood.

But where was the madman – and the axe?

Doyle looked up, blinked tears out of his eyes.

The stranger had dropped the weapon. He was pressing the palms of his hands against his temples, grimacing furiously. Perspiration had popped out on his forehead and was trickling down his reddened face.

Gasping for breath, Alex clambered to his feet and leaned back against the wall, too weak and pain-racked to move any further.

The stranger saw him. He bent down to pick up the axe, but stopped short of it. He gave a strangled cry, turned, and stumbled out of the room, out into the night and the rain.

For a long while, as he struggled to regain his breath and to overcome the pain which stitched his side, Alex was certain that he had been granted only a temporary reprieve. It made no sense for this stranger to walk away from a job so nearly finished. The man had desperately *needed* to kill Doyle. There had been nothing playful or joking about him. Each time that he had swung that axe, he had intended to sever flesh and spill blood. Certainly, he was insane. And the insane were unpredictable. But it was likewise true that a madman's violent compulsions were not easily or rapidly dissipated.

Yet the man did not return.

The pain in Doyle's side gradually eased until he could stand erect, could walk. His breath came much less raggedly than it had, although he could not inhale too deeply without amplifying the pain. His heartbeat softened and slowed.

And he was left alone.

He walked slowly to the door, his right hand

pressed to his side, and he leaned against the
frame for a moment, then stepped outside. The
rain and wind struck him with more force than
ever, chilling him.

The parking lot was deserted. The green-brown
cars sparkled with water, all still and unremark-
able.

He listened to the night.

The only sounds were the steady drumming of
the rain and the fluting of the wind along the
building.

It seemed almost as if the events in the maintenance room had been nothing but a bad dream. If
he had not had the pain in his side to convince
him of its reality, he might have gone back to look
for the axe and the other signs of what had
happened.

He walked back towards the courtyard in the
centre of the motel complex, splashing through
puddles rather than walk around them, wary of
every velvety shadow, stopping half a dozen
times to listen for imagined footsteps following
close behind him.

But there were no footsteps other than his
own.

At the top of the stairs which led to the second
level, in the northeast corner of the courtyard
overlook, he leaned against the iron safety rail to
catch his breath and to clamp down on the
renewed thump of dull pain in his side and chest.

He was cold. Deep-down cold and shivering.
The raindrops struck him like chips of ice and
melted down his face.

As he sucked the crisp air, he looked at the

dozens of identical doors and windows, all of them closed and lightless ... And he wondered, suddenly, why he had not screamed for help when the stranger had first attacked him with the axe. Even though they had been clear at the back of the motel, and even though the thunder of rain and wind was a blanket over other sounds, his voice would have carried into these rooms, would have awakened these people. If he had screamed as loudly as he could, surely someone would have come to see what was wrong. Someone would have called the police. But he had been so frightened that the thought of crying out for help had never occurred to him. The battle had been strangely noiseless, a nightmare of nearly silent thrust and counterthrust which had not reached the motel guests.

And then, remembering various newspaper stories he had read, accounts of the average man's indifference to the commission of a rape or murder in front of his eyes, Doyle wondered if anyone *would* have answered his call for help? Or would they all have turned and put pillows over their heads? Would these people in these identical rooms have reacted unemotionally and identically: with reluctance and perhaps apathy?

It was not a nice thought.

Shaking violently now, he tried to stop thinking about it as he pushed away from the rail and walked down the rain-washed promenade towards their room.

Fourteen

When Doyle finished drying his hair, Colin folded the white hotel towel and carried it into the bathroom, where he draped it over the shower rail with the rain-soaked clothes. Trying to handle himself in a calm and dignified manner – even though he was wearing only undershorts and eyeglasses, and even though he was obviously quite frightened – the boy came back into the main room and sat down in the middle of his own bed. He stared openly at Doyle's bruised right side.

Alex cautiously explored the tender flesh with the tips of his fingers, until he was satisfied that nothing was broken or so seriously damaged that it demanded a doctor's attention.

'Hurt?' Colin asked.

'Like a bitch.'

'Maybe we should get some ice to put on it.'

'It's just a bruise. Not much to be done.'

'You *think* it's just a bruise,' Colin said.

'The worst of the pain is gone already. I'll be stiff and sore for a few days, but there isn't any way to avoid that.'

'What do we do now?'

Doyle had, of course, told the boy everything

about the axe battle and the tall, gaunt man with the wild eyes. He had known that Colin would recognize a lie and would probe for the truth until he got it. This was not a child whom you could treat like a child.

Doyle stopped massaging his discoloured flesh and considered the boy's question. 'Well . . . We definitely have to change the route we'd planned on taking from here to Salt Lake City. Instead of using Route 40, we'll take either Interstate 80 or Route 24 and—'

'We changed plans before,' Colin said, blinking owlishly behind his thick, round glasses. 'And it didn't work. He picked us up again.'

'He picked us up again only when we returned to I-70, the road that *he* was using,' Doyle said. 'This time we won't go back to the main roads at all. We'll take the longer way around. We'll figure a new way into Reno from Salt Lake City – then a secondary road from Reno to San Francisco.'

Colin thought about that for a minute. 'Maybe we should stay at new motels, too. Pick them at random.'

'We have reservations and deposits waiting for us,' Doyle said.

'That's what I mean.' The boy was sombre.

'That sounds like paranoia,' Doyle said, surprised.

'I guess.'

Doyle sat up straighter against the headboard. 'You think that this character knows where we intend to stop each night?'

'He keeps picking us up in the mornings,' the boy said defensively.

'But how would he know our plans?'

Colin shrugged.

'He would have to be somebody we know,' Doyle said, not warming to the idea at all, afraid to warm to it. 'I don't know him. Do you?'

Colin just shrugged again.

'I've already described him,' Doyle said. 'A big man. Light, almost white hair, cut short. Blue eyes. Handsome. A little gaunt . . . Does he sound like somebody you know?'

'I can't tell from a description like that,' Colin said.

'Exactly. He's like ten million guys. So we'll operate under the assumption that he *is* a total stranger, and that he's just your average American madman, the kind you read about in the newspapers every day.'

'He was waiting for us in Philly.'

'Not *waiting*. He happened to—'

'He started out with us,' Colin said. 'He was right there behind us from the first.'

Doyle did not want to consider that the man might know them, might have some real or imagined grudge against them. If that were the case, this whole crazy thing would not end with the trip. If this maniac knew them, he could pick them up again in San Francisco. He could come after them any time he wanted. 'He's a stranger,' Alex insisted. 'He's nuts. I saw him in action. I saw his eyes. He is not the sort of man who could plan and execute a cross-country pursuit.'

Colin said nothing.

'And why would he pursue us? If he wants us dead – why not kill us back in Philly. Or out on the coast? Why chase us this way?'

'I don't know,' the boy admitted.

'Look, you have to accept some coincidence in this thing,' Doyle said. 'By sheer coincidence, he began his trip the same time we did, from the same block of the same street that we did. And he's crazy. A madman might very well become obsessed with a coincidence like that. He would make more of it than it was, use it as the foundation for some paranoid delusion. And everything that has happened since would explain itself.'

Colin hugged himself and rocked slowly back and forth on the bed. 'I guess you're right.'

'But you still aren't convinced.'

'No.'

Doyle sighed. 'Okay. We'll forfeit the room deposits we've made. We'll pick motels at random the next two nights – if we can find any vacancies.' He smiled, somewhat relieved even though he could not believe Colin's vague hypothesis. 'You feel better now?'

'I won't really feel better until we're in San Francisco, until we're home,' Colin said.

'That makes two of us.' Doyle slid down in bed until he was flat on his back. The movement made his bruise throb again. 'You want to turn out that light so we can catch a few winks?'

'Can you sleep after all this?' Colin asked.

'Probably not. But I'm going to try. I'm certainly not going to leave the motel now – not in the dark. And if we're going to take the back roads and add hours of driving time to our schedule, I'll need all the rest I can get.'

Colin turned out the light, but he did not slip under the covers. 'I'll just sit here awhile,' he said. 'I can't sleep now.'

'You better try.'

'I will. In a little while.'

As exhausted as he was, Doyle slept, though fitfully. He dreamed of flashing axe blades and gouting blood and maniacal laughter, and he woke repeatedly, sheathed in cold sweat. Awake, he thought about the stranger and wondered who he might be. And he thought, as well, about his own new courage. He realized that it was his love for Courtney and for Colin that had provided him with the key to this strength. When he had no one to look out for except himself, he could always run from trouble. But now . . . Well, three could not run as easily or as quickly as one. Therefore, he had been compelled to call upon resources which he had not known he possessed. Knowing, he felt more at peace with himself than he had ever been before in his life. Content, he slept. Sleeping, he dreamed again and woke with the shakes and countered the shakes with the knowledge that he could now handle the cause of them.

For two long hours Colin sat up in bed, wrapped in darkness, listening to Doyle breathe. Occasionally, the man woke from a bad dream and turned over and wrestled with the bedclothes until he could sleep again. At least he *was* dozing. Doyle's equanimity in these dangerous circumstances impressed Colin quite a bit.

Of course, he had always been impressed with Alex Doyle – more than he had ever been able to

let the man know. Sometimes he wanted to grab
hold of Doyle and hug him and hold on to him
forever. He was afraid, all through the courtship,
that Courtney would lose Doyle. He knew how
much they cared for each other and suspected the
intensity of their physical relationship, yet he had
been sure Doyle would leave them. Now that
Doyle was theirs, he wanted to hug him and be
around him and learn from him. But he was not
capable of that hug, for it seemed too juvenile a
means of expressing what he felt. He had worked
too hard and too long at being an adult to let
himself slip now, no matter how much he loved,
liked, and admired Alex Doyle. Therefore, he had
to let his feelings be known in small ways, in
hundreds of separate, simple gestures that would
say it all as well as that one hug would say it, if
less forcefully.

He got off his bed when the first morning light
found its way around the edges of the heavy
curtains, and he went into the bathroom to
shower. With Alex in the room beyond, with the
warm water cascading down on him and the
yellow soap foaming pleasantly against his thin
limbs, Colin worried less and less about the
stranger in the Chevrolet van. With just a little bit
of luck, everything would be fine. It *had* to come
out all right in the end, because Alex Doyle was
here to make certain that nothing really bad
happened to him or to Courtney.

By the time George Leland reached the Automover which was parked near the front of the
Rockies Motor Hotel, he had forgotten all about

Doyle and the boy. He fumbled with his keys, dropped them. He pawed clumsily in an inch-deep puddle until he found them again. Unlocking the cab door, he climbed into the truck, unable to recall the silent chase through the motel corridors or the axe-swinging madness in the maintenance room when he had come within seconds and inches of killing a man. He was too beaten down with pain to care about this sudden amnesia.

It was the worst headache yet. The pain was most fierce in and around the right eye, but now it also fanned out across his entire forehead and back to the top of his skull. It brought tears to his eyes. He could even hear his teeth grinding together like sandstone wheels, but he could not stop the hard, involuntary chewing motion; it was as if he were possessed, as if his possessor thought that the pain could be masticated, shredded into fine pieces, swallowed, and digested away.

There had been no warning signs. Usually, at least one hour in advance of the first wave of pain, he grew dizzy and nauseated, and he saw that spiral of hot multi-coloured light turning around and around behind his eye. But not tonight. One moment he had felt just fine, even exhilarated, and the next, pain had hit him like a hammer blow. It had been an ugly but comparatively small pain to begin with – hadn't it? A small pain at the start? He could not remember exactly where he had been when it first struck him, but he was sure the pain had been only mild, initially. Certainly bearable. However, it had rapidly got worse until, now, he despaired of reaching his own motel before he was completely incapacitated.

He drove out of the motel lot, slammed off a four-inch kerb and on to the highway, the van's springs squealing beneath him. He did not feel like a part of the vehicle tonight. He was no extension of it. He had lost his usual empathy with machines. He was a stranger in this contraption, and the steering wheel felt like an alien artifact, an inhuman device, under his large hands.

He squinted at the wet pavement as he drove, tried to push back the rain and the ghostly tendrils of fog.

A low, sleek car approached from the opposite direction, flashed past in a violent spray of water. Its four headlights were much too bright; they sliced into Leland's eyes like a quartet of knives and drew a painful wound across his forehead.

Unconsciously he pulled the wheel hard to the right, away from the light which so offended him. The van crunched on to the shoulder of the road, nosed down, bounced in a rut, came up again with a prolonged shudder. In the cargo hold, furniture shifted noisily. Suddenly, immediately ahead, a waist-high brown-brick wall looked out of the night, stark and deadly. Leland cried out and wheeled hard to the left. The right front fender nicked the bricks. Then the Chevrolet jumped back on to the road, sliding in the rainwater for a long, dangerous moment before it finally, reluctantly, came back under his control.

He reached the motel only because he encountered no other traffic. If even one other car had passed him, he would have demolished the Chevrolet and killed himself.

At the door of his room, rain beating against his back, he had trouble inserting the key in the lock, and he cursed nearly loudly enough to wake the other guests.

Inside, as he closed the door, the pain abruptly worsened, driving him to his knees on the stained carpet. He was sure that he was dying.

But the new pain passed, and the agony became merely unbearable again.

He went to bed and almost lay down before he realised that he had to get out of his clothes first. They were wet clear through. If he passed the rest of the night in them, he would be ill in the morning ... Slowly, with exaggerated movements, he undressed and dried himself on the tufted bedspread. Even then, he was chilled to the bone. Trembling, he got into bed and pulled the cover up to his chin. He gave himself over to the unrelenting pain and tried to ride with it.

It lasted more than twice as long as usual. And when, well after dawn, it was finally gone, the nightmares which always followed it were also worse than they had ever been. The only lovely thing in that parade of grisly images was Courtney. She kept popping up. Nude and beautiful. Her full, round breasts and delightfully long legs were welcome relief from the other visions ... Yet, each time that she did appear in the dreams, an imaginary dream-Leland killed her with an imaginary knife. And the murder was, without exception, curiously satisfying.

Thursday

Fifteen

Interstate 25 ran north from Denver and connected with Interstate 80 just inside the Wyoming border. That was all well-paved, four-lane, controlled access highway that would carry them straight into San Francisco without a single intersection to get in the way.

But they did not take it, because it seemed like too obvious an alternative to the route which they had originally planned to use. If the madman in the Chevrolet van *had* become obsessed with them — and with killing them — then he might make the effort to think one step ahead of them. And if he realized that they would now leave their preplanned route, he would see, with one quick glance at a map, that I-25 and I-80 was their next best bet.

'So we'll take Route 24,' Doyle said.

'What kind of road is it?' Colin asked, leaning across the seat to look at the map which Doyle had propped against the steering wheel.

'Pieces of it are four-lane. Most of it isn't.'

Colin reached out and traced it with one finger. Then he pointed to the grey-shaded areas. 'Mountains?'

'Some. High plateaus. But there are a good

many deserts, alkali and salt flats . . .'

'I'm glad we've got air conditioning.'

Doyle folded the map and handed it to the boy. 'Belt yourself in.'

Colin put the map in the glove compartment, then did as he had been told. As Doyle drove out of the Rockies Motor Hotel parking lot, the boy tucked in his orange-and-black Phantom of the Opera T-shirt, smoothed the wrinkles out of the phantom's hideously deformed face, and took a couple of minutes to comb his thick brown hair until it fell straight to his shoulders just the way he liked it. Then he sat up straight and watched the sun-scorched landscape whisk past as the mountains drew nearer.

The electric-blue sky was streaked with narrow bands of grey-white clouds, but it was no longer a storm sky. Last night's downpour had ended as abruptly as it had begun, leaving few traces. The sandy soil alongside the road looked almost parched, dusty.

The traffic was not heavy this morning, and what there was of it moved so well and orderly that Doyle did not have to pass a single car all the way out of the Denver area.

And there was no van behind them.

'You're awfully quiet this morning,' Alex said after fifteen minutes had passed in silence. He glanced away from the twisting snakes of hot air that danced above the highway, looked at the boy. 'You feeling okay?'

'I was thinking.'

'You're *always* thinking.'

'I was thinking about this – maniac.'

'And?'

'We aren't being followed, are we?'

'No.'

Colin nodded. 'I bet we never see him again.'

Doyle frowned, accelerated slightly to keep up with the flow of cars around them. 'How can you be so sure?'

'Just a hunch.'

'I see. I thought you might have a theory . . .'

'No. Only a hunch.'

'Well,' Doyle said, 'I'd feel a whole lot better if you *did* have some reasons for thinking we've seen the last of him.'

'So would I,' the boy said.

Even as he drove into the parking lot that encircled the Rockies Motor Hotel, George Leland knew that he had missed them. The headache had been so damned long and intense . . . And the period of unconsciousness, afterward, had lasted at least two hours. They might not be too far out in front of him, but they had surely gotten a head start.

The Thunderbird was not where it had been the night before. That space was empty.

He refused to panic. Nothing was lost. They had not escaped. *He knew exactly where they were going.*

He parked where the Thunderbird had been, cut off the engine. There was a map on top of the same tissue box which held the .32-calibre pistol. Leland unfolded it on the seat and turned sideways to study it, traced the meagre system of highways that crossed Colorado and Utah.

'They don't have many choices,' he told the golden girl in the seat next to him. 'Either they stay on the planned route – or they take one of these other two.'

She said nothing.

'After last night, they'll change their plans.'

When his headache was gone, Leland had also lost his selective amnesia. He could now recall everything: arriving at the motel an hour before they did, watching the lobby until they arrived, cautiously following them to their room, coming back in the middle of the night and trying to pick the lock on their door, the silent chase, and the axe . . . If that damned headache had only held off for a few minutes, if it had not come on him when it did, he would have finished off Alex Doyle.

Leland was not disturbed by the realization that he had tried to kill a man. After suffering so much at the hands of others, he had finally come to understand that there was only one thing that would destroy this far-reaching conspiracy that was working against him: force, violence, counter-attack. He must smash this entire evil association which had been formed solely to drive him to complete despair. And since Alex Doyle – and the boy, as well – formed the keystone of this conspiracy, murder was quite justified. He had acted in self-defence.

On Monday, when he had caught sight of his own eyes in the mirror, he had been confused, shocked by what he saw. Now, when he looked in the mirror, he saw nothing but a reflection, a flat image. After all, he was only doing what Court-ney wanted, so that they could be together again, so that everything could be as wonderful as it had been two years ago.

'They can either go up to Wyoming and catch Interstate 80, or go southwest on Route 24. What do you think?'

'Whatever you say, George,' the golden girl replied, her voice faint but pleasant, like a happy memory.

Leland studied the map for several minutes. 'Damn . . . They probably went up and caught I-80 outside of Cheyenne. But even if they did, and even if we went that way and managed to catch up with them, we wouldn't be able to do anything to them. That's a major highway. Too much traffic, too many police patrols. All we could do would be follow them – and that's not enough.' He was quiet for a while, thinking. 'But if they went the other way, it's a whole different ballgame. That's desolate country. Not as much traffic. Fewer cops. We could really make up for lost time. Might get a chance at them somewhere along the way.'

She waited, silently.

'We'll take Route 24,' he said at last. 'And if they *did* go the other way . . . Well, we can always pick them up again tonight, at their motel.'

She said nothing.

He smiled at her, folded the map and placed it on top of the tissue box, where it covered the blue-grey pistol.

He started the van.

He drove away from the Rockies Motor Hotel and then from Denver, going southwest towards Utah.

* * *

During the morning they came out of the mountains and down the piney valleys of Colorado, from winter's leftover snow to sun and sand again. They went through Rifle and Debeque, crossing the Colorado River twice, then passed Grand Junction and, soon after, the border. In Utah, the mountains fell back into the distance and the land became sandier, and there was less traffic than there had been. For long minutes theirs was the only car in sight on the level stretches of open road.

'What if we had a flat tyre now?' Colin asked, indicating the vistas of unpopulated land.

'We won't.'

'We might.'

'We have all new tyres,' Doyle said.

'But what if?'

'Then we'd change it.'

'And if the spare went flat too?'

'We'd fix it.'

'How?'

Alex realized that they were playing one of the boy's games and he smiled. Maybe the kid's hunch was a good one. Maybe it was all over now. Perhaps they could yet restore to the trip that fun which they had known at the beginning of it. 'In the emergency kit in the trunk of this car,' Doyle said in an exaggerated professional voice, 'there is a large spraycan which you attach to the valve of the flat tyre. It inflates the tyre and simultaneously seals the puncture. You will then be able to drive until you locate a service station which will attend to your needs.'

'Pretty clever.'

'Isn't it?'

Colin held an imaginary aerosol dispenser in one hand, pushed on the unseen button, and made a sputtering noise. 'But what if the spraycan doesn't work?'

'Oh, it will.'

'Okay . . . But what if we have *three* flats?'

Doyle laughed.

'It could happen,' Colin said.

'Sure. And we could have *four* flats.'

'And what would we do?'

As Doyle started to tell him that they would get out of the car and walk, a horn blared behind them. It was loud and close and uncomfortably familiar. It was the van.

Sixteen

Before Alex could react properly, before the fear could well up and he could tramp down on the accelerator and rocket away from the Automover, the van swung into the left-hand lane and started to go round him, its strident horn still wailing. Far out ahead on the grey, heat-twisted road – clear to the high, rocky, multi-layered Capitol Reefs which stood miles away – there was not any eastbound traffic to get in the van's path.

'You can't let him go round us!' Colin said.

'I know.'

If the bastard got out in front of them, he would be able to blockade the entire roadway. The cracked stone shoulders on both sides were too narrow and the sand beyond them too dry and soft and loose for the Thunderbird to leave the pavement and regain the lead once that was lost.

Doyle put his foot down.

The big car surged ahead.

But the stranger in the van, though mad, was not stupid. He had been expecting that man-oeuvre. He had put speed on too, and at least for the moment, he was able to stay even with Doyle.

Wind roared between the two parallel vehicles as they hurtled westward.

'We'll outpace him,' Alex said.

Colin did not respond.

The slim speedometer needle climbed smoothly to eighty and then up to eighty-five. Doyle glanced at it once. Tense and frightened, Colin watched it with real dread.

The flat land whipped past them in a shimmering white blur of sand and heat and free-lying salt.

And the Automover hung beside them.

'He can't keep it up,' Alex said.

Ninety. Ninety-five . . .

Then, as they were rushing towards a hundred-miles-an-hour, with the wind whooping between them, the madman pulled his wheel to the right. Not much. Just a little bit. And only for an instant. The whole side of the Automover made light, brief contact with the full length of the Thunderbird.

Sparks showered up and skittered like a fall of bright stars across the windshield in front of Doyle. Tortured sheet metal screamed and coughed and crumpled up on itself.

The steering wheel was nearly torn out of Doyle's hand. He grappled with it, held on as the car lurched onto the stone shoulder, kicking up gravel that rattled noisily in the undercarriage. Their speed fell, and they began a slow sideways turn. Alex was certain that they were going to plough into the van, which was still alongside of them. But then the car began to right itself . . . He took them back onto the highway, touching the gas pedal when he would have preferred to go with the brakes.

'You all right?' he asked Colin.

The boy swallowed hard. 'Yes.'

'Better hold on, then. We're going to get the hell out of here,' he said as the Thunderbird gradually picked up the speed which it had lost, casting its pale shadow on the side of the Chevrolet.

Doyle risked one quick glance away from the road, looked up at the van's side window, which was no more than three or four feet away. Despite the short distance between them, he could not see the other driver, not even his silhouette. The man was sitting up higher than Doyle, on the far side of the cab, and he was very well hidden by the yellow-white desert sunlight that played upon the window glass.

Eighty miles an hour again, making up for lost time and for lost ground. And now on up to eighty-five, with the speedometer needle quivering slightly. It hesitated on the eighty-five; in fact, for a moment it looked as if it would stick there, and then it jerked and rose slowly.

Alex watched the Chevrolet out of the corner of his eye. When he first sensed it moving in to brush against them a second time, he would take the car onto the stony burm and try to avoid another collision. They could not tolerate much more of that banging around. Though it was half again as expensive as the Automover van, the big luxury car would come apart much sooner and more completely than the Chevrolet. It would dissolve around them like a flimsy paper construction, roll over and over like a weightless model, and burn faster than a cardboard carton.

At ninety miles an hour, the car began to shake

badly, making a noise like stones rolling in the bottom of a washtub. The steering wheel vibrated furiously in Doyle's hands. And then, worse, it started to spin uselessly back and forth.

Doyle eased up on the accelerator, although that was the last thing he wanted to do.

The needle fell. At eighty-five, the ride was smooth and the car was under control.

'Something's broken!' Colin shouted over the roar of the wind and the two competing engines.

'No. It must have been a section of bad road.'

Though he knew that their luck was not running that way, Alex hoped to God that what he had told the boy was true. Let it be true. Let it be nothing more serious than a piece of bad road, a section of rain-runnelled pavement. Don't let anything happen to the Thunderbird. It must not break down. They must not be stranded out here in the sand and the salt flats, not alone, not so far from help, and now with the madman as their only company.

He tried the accelerator.

The car picked up, hit ninety . . .

And the violent shudder returned, as if the frame and body were no longer firmly joined and were slamming into each other, parting, slamming together again. This time, as he lost control of the wheel, he felt the horrible quaking in the gas pedal as well. Their top speed was going to be eighty-five. Otherwise, the car would fall apart. Therefore, they were not going to outpace the Chevrolet.

The driver of the van seemed to realize this the

same moment that Doyle did. He tooted his horn, then pulled away from them out in front where he had command of the highway.

'What are we going to do?' asked Colin.

'Wait and see what *he* does.'

When the Automover was approximately a thousand yards out ahead of them, wrapped up in the deceptively undulating streams of hot air that were rising off the superheated road, it slowed down to a steady eighty-five and maintained a consistent half-mile lead.

A mile passed.

On both sides of the road, the land became even whiter, as if it had been bleached by the raw sun. It was punctuated only by rare, ugly clumps of struggling scrub and by occasional dark rock teeth that were all stained and rotted by the desert wind and heat.

Two miles.

The van was still out there, taunting them.

The dashboard vents spewed crisp, cold air, and still the interior of the Thunderbird was too warm and close. Alex felt perspiration bead on his forehead. His shirt was sticking to him.

Three miles.

'Maybe we should stop,' Colin said.

'And turn back?'

'Maybe.'

'He would see us,' Doyle said. 'He would turn right around and follow – and before long, he'd be out in front of us again.'

'Well . . .'

'Let's wait and see what he does,' Doyle said again, trying to keep the fear out of his voice. He was aware that the boy needed an example of strength. 'You want to get the map and see how far it is to the next town?'

Colin understood the significance of the question. He grabbed the map and opened it on his knees. It covered him like a quilt. Squinting through his Coke-bottle glasses, he found their last known position, estimated the distance they had come since then, and marked the spot with one finger. He located the nearest town, checked the key at the bottom of the map, then did some figuring in his head.

'Well?' Doyle asked.

'Sixty miles.'

'You sure?'

'Positive.'

'I see.'

It was too damned far.

Colin folded the map and put it away. He sat like a stone sculpture, staring at the back of the Chevrolet van.

The highway crested a gentle slope, dropped away into a broad alkali basin. It looked like an ink line drawn across a clean sheet of typewriter paper. For miles and miles to the west, the road was empty. Nothing moved out there.

This complete isolation was precisely what the driver of the van wanted. He braked hard, pulled the Chevrolet toward the right burm, then swung it around to the left in a broad loop. The van stopped, sideways in the road, blocking most of both lanes.

Doyle tapped the brakes, then realized that there was no percentage in slowing down or stopping altogether. He put his foot on the accelerator again. 'Here we go!'

Holding a steady eighty-five, the Thunderbird bore down on the van, aimed straight at the centre of the green-and-blue advertisement painted on its flank. Seven hundred yards lay between them. Now only six hundred – five, four, three hundred . . .

'He isn't going to move!' Colin said.

'Doesn't matter.'

'We'll hit!'

'No.'

'Alex—'

Fifty yards from the truck, Doyle wheeled to the right. Tyres squealed. The car rushed across the gravelled burm, bounced as wildly as if the springs had turned to rubber, and kept on going.

Doyle realized that he was attempting to pull off a stunt which only a short while ago he had thought impossible. Now, whether it was possible or not, it was their only hope. He was terrified.

The car ploughed into the grainy white soil that edged the highway, and alkali dust plumed up behind them like a vapour trail. Their speed was cut by a third in the first few seconds, and the Thunderbird lurched sickeningly in the sandy earth.

It'll stop us, Doyle thought. We'll be stranded here.

He stomped the accelerator to the floor.

Although they were still doing better than fifty, the wide tyres protested the loss of traction, spun furiously. The car slewed sideways, fishtailed back before picking up the speed demanded of it.

They passed the Automover.

Doyle angled back towards the highway. He kept the accelerator pressed all the way down. Through the partially unresponsive steering wheel, he felt the treacherous land shifting beneath them. However, before the sand could capture one or more of the wheels, they reached the shoulder of the road and kicked up hundreds of small stones as they plunged back onto the road.

In seconds, they were doing eighty-five again, heading west, the van behind them.

'You did it!' Colin said.

'Not yet.'

'But you did it!' He was still frightened, but he also sounded pleasantly excited.

Doyle looked in the mirror.

Far back there, the van was starting after them, a white speck against the whiter land.

'He's coming?' Colin asked.

'Yes.'

'See if it'll go past ninety now.'

Doyle tried, but the car began to shake and rattle. 'No good. Something was damaged when he slammed into us.'

'Well, at least we know you can drive us around any roadblock he throws up,' the boy said.

Doyle looked at him. 'You've got more faith in my driving than I do. That was pretty hairy back there.'

'You can do it,' Colin said. Desert sunlight, coming through the window, made his wire-frame glasses look like tiny tubes of light.

Three minutes later the van was on their tail.

But when it tried to come round them, Doyle

swung the Thunderbird into the left-hand lane, blocking the van and forcing it to fall back. When the Chevy attempted to move in on the right, Doyle weaved in front of it and blew his own horn to counter the other's savage blaring.

For several minutes and miles they played that game with an unsportsmanlike disregard for rules, cruising from one side of the road to the other. Then inevitably, the van found an opening and took advantage of it, drawing even with them.

'Here we go again,' Doyle said.

As if he had cued it, the Automover closed the space between them and brushed the car. Sparks showered up and sputtered out in an instant, and metal whined, though not as loudly or as gratingly as it had the first time that they had collided.

Alex fought the wheel. They plummeted along the gravel shoulder for a thousand yards before he could get them back onto the highway.

The van hit them again, harder than before.

This time Alex lost control. He could not hold onto the sweat-slicked steering wheel which spun through his hands. It was as slippery as a stick of butter. Only when they were off the road, grinding crazily through the ridged sand, was he able to get a good grip on the wet plastic and regain command of their fates.

They were doing forty-five when they came back onto the road, and they were a few yards ahead of the van. But it caught up with them a moment later and hung beside them until they were doing eighty-five again. The whole right side of the Automover was scraped and dented.

Doyle knew, as he looked anxiously at the other vehicle, that the left side of the Thunderbird was in much worse condition.

The van swept in at them again. There was a sudden *bang*! so loud that Alex thought they had been hit a fourth time. However, there was no impact with the sound. And, abruptly, the Chevrolet lost speed, fell behind them.

'What's he doing?' Colin asked.

It was too good to be true, Doyle thought. 'One of his tyres blew.'

'You're kidding.'

'I'm not kidding.'

The boy slumped back against the seat, pale and shaking, limping, wrung out. In a thin, almost whispered voice, he said, '*Jesus*!'

Seventeen

The town survived despite the inhospitable land in which it stood. The low buildings – whether they were of wood, brick, or stone – had all turned a dull yellow-brown in order to coexist with the merciless sun and the wind-blown sand. Here and there, alkaline encrustations limed the edges of walls, but that was the only variation in the drabness. The main highway – which became the borough's most important street – had been a harsh grey-black line through the desert ever since they had crossed over from Colorado; but now it succumbed to the influence of the town, became dun and dusty. Out on the open land, the wind had scoured the road clean; but here, the buildings blocked the wind and let the dust collect. A soft powder filmed the automobiles, taking the shine out of them. The dust seemed like the hands of the loving desert, gradually stealing back this meagre plot which men had taken from it.

The police station, three blocks west along the main street, was as dreary as everything else, a one-storey building that was losing the mortar between its mustard-coloured stones.

The officer in charge of the station, a man who

called himself Captain Ackridge, wore a brown uniform that fitted in with his town and a hard, experienced face which did not. He was six-foot, two hundred pounds, perhaps ten years older than Doyle but with a body ten years younger. His close-cropped hair was black, his eyes darker than that. He held himself like a soldier on parade, stiff and proud.

He came out and looked at the Thunderbird. He walked the whole way round it and seemed to be as interested in the undamaged angles as he was in the long scars down the driver's side. He leaned close to the tinted windshield and peered in at Colin as if the boy were a fish in an aquarium. Then he looked at the damage on the car's left side again and was satisfied with his inspection.

'Come on back inside,' he told Doyle. His voice was crisp and precise in spite of the underlying Southwest accent. 'We'll talk about it.'

They returned to the station, crossed the public room where two secretaries were pounding on typewriters and one uniformed, overweight cop was taking a coffee break and munching on an eclair. They went through the door to Ackridge's office, and the big man closed it behind them.

'What do you think can be done?' Alex asked as Ackridge went around behind his neatly ordered desk.

'Have a seat.'

Doyle went to the chair that faced the scarred metal desk, but he did not sit down. 'Look, that flat tyre won't slow the bastard up for long. And if he—'

'Please sit down, Mr Doyle,' the policeman said, sitting down himself. His well-worn spring-backed chair squeaked as if there were a live mouse in the cushion.

Somewhat irritated, Doyle sat down. 'I think—'

'Let's just do this my way,' Ackridge said, smiling briefly. It was an imitation smile, utterly false. The policeman seemed to understand that it was a bad copy, for he gave it up right away. 'You have some identification?'

'Me?'

'It was you I asked.'

The officer's voice contained no real malice, yet it chilled Doyle. He got his wallet from his hip pocket, withdrew his driver's licence from one of the plastic windows, and pushed it across the desk.

The policeman studied it. 'Doyle.'

'That's right.'

'Philadelphia.'

'Yes, but we're moving to San Francisco. Of course, I don't have my California licence yet.' He knew he was on the verge of babbling, his tongue loosened not so much by the residual fear of their encounter with the madman in the van as by Ackridge's penetrating black eyes.

'You have an owner's card for that T-Bird?'

Doyle found it, held the wallet open to the proper plastic envelope, and passed the whole thing over to the policeman.

Ackridge looked at it for a long time. The billfold was small in his large, hard hands. 'First Thunderbird you've owned?'

Alex could not see what that had to do with

anything, but he answered the question anyway. 'Second.'

'Occupation?'

'Mine? Commercial artist.'

Ackridge looked up at him, seemed to stare through him. 'Exactly what is that?'

'I do advertising work,' Doyle said.

'And you get paid well for that?'

'Pretty well,' Doyle said.

Ackridge started to leaf through the other cards in the wallet, taking a couple of seconds with each. His sober, intense interest in these private things was almost obscene.

What in the hell is going on here? Doyle wondered. I came here to report a crime. I'm a good, upstanding citizen – not a suspect!

He cleared his throat. 'Excuse me, Captain.'

Ackridge stopped flipping through the cards. 'What is it?'

Last night, Doyle told himself, I faced a man who was trying to kill me with an axe. Today I can surely face this two-bit police chief.

'Captain,' he said, 'I don't see why you're so interested in who I am. Isn't the most important thing – well, going after this man in the Auto-mover?'

'I always believe it pays to know the victim as well as the victimiser,' Ackridge said. With that, he went back to the cards in Doyle's wallet.

It was all wrong. How on earth could it have gone sour like this – and why had it?

So that he would not be humiliated by watching the cop prying through his wallet, Alex looked around the room. The walls were

186

institutional-grey and brightened by only three
things: a poster-sized framed photograph of the
President of the United States; an equally large
photograph of the late J. Edgar Hoover; and a
four-foot-square map of the immediate area.
Filing cabinets stood side by side along one wall,
breaking only for a window and an air-
conditioning unit. There were three straight-
backed chairs, the desk, the chair in which
Ackridge sat, and a flagstand bearing a full-size
cotton-and-silk Old Glory.

'Conscientious objector?' Ackridge asked.

Alex looked at him, surprised. 'What did you
say?'

Ackridge showed him the selective service card
in his wallet. 'You have a CO rating here.'

Why had he ever kept that card? He was under
no legal obligation to carry it with him, especially
not now that he was thirty years old. They had
long ago stopped drafting men over twenty-six.
Indeed, the draft was pretty much of a forgotten
thing for *everyone*. Yet he had transferred the
card from one billfold to the next – through
maybe three or four of them. Why? Subcon-
sciously had he believed that possession of the
card was proof that his non-violent philosophy was
based on principle and not cowardice? Or had he
simply given in to that common American neuro-
sis – the reluctance and sometimes the inability to
throw away anything with a vaguely official look
to it, no matter how dated it might be?

'I did alternate service in a veterans' hospital,'
Doyle said, though he did not feel the need to
justify himself to Ackridge.

'I was too young for Korea and too old for Nam,' the cop said. 'But I served in the regular army, in-between wars.' He handed back the driver's licence and the wallet.

Alex put the licence in the wallet, the wallet in his pocket, and he said, 'About the man in the Chevrolet—'

'You ever try marijuana?' Ackridge asked.

Easy, Doyle thought. Be damn careful. Be damn nice.

'Long time ago,' he told the cop. He no longer tried to find a way to get back to the man in the Automover, because he saw that for whatever reason, Ackridge didn't care about that.

'Still use it?'

'No.'

Ackridge smiled. It was the same bad imitation. 'Even if you did use it every day of the week, you wouldn't tell a crusty old cop like me.'

'I'm telling the truth,' Doyle said, feeling new perspiration on his forehead.

'Other things?'

'What do you mean?'

Leaning across the desk, his voice lowered to a melodramatic whisper, Ackridge said, 'Barbiturates, amphetamines, LSD, cocaine . . .'

'Drugs are for people who don't really care for life,' Doyle said. He believed what he was saying, but he knew it must sound hollow to the cop. 'I happen to love life. I don't need drugs. I can make myself happy without them.'

Ackridge watched him closely for a moment, then leaned back in his chair, crossed his heavy arms on his chest. 'You want to know why I'm asking all these questions?'

Alex did not respond, for he was not sure whether or not he wanted to know.

'I'll tell you,' Ackridge said. 'I've got two theories about this story of yours – about the man in the Automover. First one is – none of it happened. You hallucinated it all. Could be. Could be like that. If you were really high on something, maybe LSD, you could have given yourself a real bad spook.'

The thing to do, was just to listen. Don't argue. Just let him go on and, hopefully, get out of here as soon as possible. Still, Alex could not help saying, 'What about the side of my car? The paint's gone. The body is all torn up. My door won't open . . .'

'I'm not saying *that* is imaginary,' Ackridge told him. 'But it could be that you side-swiped a retaining wall or an outcropping of rock – anything.'

'Ask Colin,' Doyle said.

'The boy in the car? Your – brother-in-law?'

'Yes.'

'How old is he?'

'Eleven.'

Ackridge shook his burly head. 'He's too young for me to touch. And he'd probably just say anything he supposed you wanted him to say.'

Alex cleared his throat, which was tight and dry. 'Search the car. You won't find any drugs.'

'Well,' Ackridge said, purposefully emphasizing his drawl, 'let me tell you my other theory before you go getting your dander up. I think it's a better one, anyway. Know what it is?'

'No.'

'I think maybe you were tooling along in that big black cars of yours, playing the king of the road, and you passed some local boy who was driving the only broken-down old pickup he could afford.' Ackridge smiled again, and this time it was a genuine smile. 'He probably looked at you with your loud clothes and long hair and effeminate ways, and he wondered why you could have the big car while he had to settle for the truck. And, naturally, the more he thought about it, the madder he got. So he caught up with you and held a little duel on the highway. Couldn't have hurt his old wreck. You were the only one with something fancy to lose.'

'Why would I tell you it was an Automover? Why would I make up an elaborate story about a cross-country pursuit?' Doyle asked, barely able to control his anger but painfully aware that any expression of it would land him in jail, or worse.

'That's easy.'

'I'd like to hear it.'

Ackridge stood up and pushed his chair back, walked over and stood by the flag, his hands clasped behind his back. 'You figured that I might not go after a local boy, that I'd favour one of ours over someone like you. So you made up this other thing to get me onto the case. Once I'd gone on record, started a full investigation, I couldn't have backed out of it so easily when I learned the real story.'

'This is far-fetched,' Doyle said. 'And you know it.'

'Sounds reasonable to me.'

Alex got to his feet, his damp hands fisted at his sides. Once it had been easy for him to take this kind of abuse and crawl away without another thought. But now, with the changes that had taken place in him during the last couple of days, excessive humility was not his best suit. 'Then you aren't going to help us?'

Ackridge looked at him with real hatred now. For the first time there was genuine malice in his voice. 'I'm not a man you can call a pig one day – then run to for help the next.'

'I've never called any policeman a pig,' Alex said.

But the cop was not listening. He appeared to be looking straight through Doyle when he said, 'For fifteen years or better, this country's been like a sick man. It's been absolutely delirious, staggering around and bumping into things, not sure where it was or where it was going or even if it would survive. But it isn't so sick any more. It's casting off the parasites that made it ill. Soon there won't be any parasites at all.'

'I get you,' Alex said, shaking uncontrollably with both fear and rage.

'It will up and kill *all* the germs and be as healthy as it once was,' Ackridge said, grinning broadly, hands still clasped behind his back, rocking on his heels.

'I understand you perfectly,' Alex said. 'May I leave?'

Ackridge laughed in short, sharp barks. 'Leave? Gee, I really would appreciate it if you did.'

* * *

Colin climbed out of the car and let Alex slide inside, then followed him and pulled the door shut, locked it. 'Well?'

Alex gripped the steering wheel as hard as he could and stared at his whitened knuckles. 'Captain Ackridge thinks I might have been taking drugs and imagined the whole thing.'

'Oh, great.'

'Or maybe some local boys were harassing us in a pickup. He sure doesn't want to favour us over some good old boys having their fun.'

Colin buckled his seatbelt. 'Was it really that bad?'

'I think he'd have jailed me if you hadn't been along,' Doyle said. 'He didn't know what to do with an eleven-year-old boy.'

'What now?' He pulled at his Phantom of the Opera T-shirt.

'We'll fill the gas tank,' Alex said. 'Buy some take-out food, and drive straight through to Reno.'

'What about Salt Lake City?'

'We'll skip it,' Doyle said. 'I want to get to San Francisco as soon as I can – and get as far off our schedule as possible, in case that bastard *does* know our route.'

'Reno isn't just around the corner,' the boy said, remembering how far it had seemed on the map. 'How long will it take us to get there?'

Doyle surveyed the dusty street, the yellow-brown buildings, and the alkali-skimmed automobiles. These were all inanimate objects without intentions of their own, malevolent or otherwise. Yet he feared and hated them. 'I could get us into Reno a little after dawn tomorrow.'

'Without sleeping?'

'I won't sleep tonight anyway.'

'Driving will wear you out, though. No matter how you feel now, you'll fall asleep at the wheel.'

'No,' Alex said. 'If I feel like nodding off, I'll pull over to the side of the road and take a fifteen- or twenty-minute nap.'

'What about the maniac?' the boy asked, jerking a thumb towards the road behind him.

'That flat tyre will slow him up some. It won't be easy handling the van by himself, jacking it up . . . And once he's on the road again, he won't drive all night. He'll figure that we stopped at a motel somewhere. If he knows we planned to be in Salt Lake City tonight – and I still don't see *how* he could know – then he'll be up there looking for us. We can get away from him for good, this time.' He started the car. 'If the T-bird holds together, that is.'

'Want me to plan a route?' Colin asked.

Alex nodded. 'Back roads. But roads we can make decent time on.'

'This might even be fun,' Colin said, opening the map once more. 'A real adventure.'

Doyle looked at him, incredulous. Then he saw, in the boy's eyes, a haunted look that must have matched his own, and he realized that the statement had been sheer bravado. Colin was trying as best he could to stand up under the incredible stress – and he was doing remarkably well for an eleven-year-old.

'You're really something else,' Doyle said.

Colin blushed. 'You too.'

'We make quite a pair.'

'Don't we?'

'Zooming off into the unknown,' Alex said, 'without even blinking an eye. Wilbur and Orville.'

'Lewis and Clark,' the boy said, grinning.

'Columbus and – Hudson.'

'Abbott and Costello,' Colin said.

It might have been just the circumstances, but Doyle thought that was the funniest line he had heard in years. It brought tears to his eyes. 'Laurel and Hardy,' he said when he was finished laughing. He put the car in gear and drove away from the police station.

The van was as difficult to handle as a stubborn cow. After half an hour of constant struggle, Leland got the wheels blocked and the jack pumped up enough to remove the punctured tyre. The wind coming across the sand flats made the Chevy sway lightly on its metal crutch. And if the furniture in the cargo hold shifted without warning . . .

An hour after he had begun, Leland tightened the last nut on the spare and let the van down again. When he heaved the ruined tyre into the truck, he realized he should stop at the first service station to get it repaired. But . . .

Doyle and the kid had gotten too much of a head start already. Though it was true that he could pick them up again tonight in Salt Lake City, he did not want to lose the chance of finishing them out here on the open road. The closer they got to San Francisco, the less sure he was of himself and his ability to dispose of them.

And if he didn't get them out of the picture, what would Courtney think? Courtney was depending on him. If he didn't take care of those two, then he and Courtney could never be together like they wanted.

Therefore, the tyre could wait.

He closed the rear doors of the van, locked them, and went around to the cab. Five minutes later he was doing ninety-five on the flat, deserted highway.

Detective Ernie Hoval of the Ohio State Police ate supper in an interchange diner which most of the cops in the area favoured. The atmosphere was pretty bad, but the food was good. And policemen were given a twenty percent discount.

He was halfway through his club sandwich and French fries when the sallow, smart-ass lab technician sat down in the other half of the booth, facing him. 'Do you mind some company?' the man asked.

Hoval winced. He did mind, but he shrugged.

'I didn't know a man like you took advantage of thinly disguised bribes like restaurant discounts,' the technician said, opening the menu which the waitress brought him.

'I didn't when I first started,' Hoval said, surprised to find that he actually *wanted* to talk to this man. 'But everyone else does . . . And there's not much else you can take advantage of – if you want to keep being a good cop.'

'Ah, you're just like all the rest of us,' the technician said, dismissing Hoval with a brisk wave of the hand.

'Poor.'

The other man's pale face crinkled in a grin, and he even allowed himself a soft laugh. 'How's the club sandwich?'

'Fine,' Hoval said, around a mouthful of it.

The technician ordered one, without French fries, and a coffee. When the girl had gone, he said, 'What about the Pulham investigation?'

'I'm not on it full time now,' Hoval said.

'Oh?'

'Not much I can do,' Hoval explained. 'If the killer was going to California in an Automover, he's way out of my territory. The FBI is checking on the names they got from Automover's central records. They've narrowed it down to a few dozen. Looks like maybe a couple of weeks until they find our guy.'

The technician frowned, picked up the salt shaker and turned it around and around in his bony hands. 'A couple of weeks could be too late. When a fruitcake starts to go, he goes fast.'

'You still on that kick?' Hoval asked, putting down his sandwich.

'I think we're dealing with a pyschotic. And if we are, he'll add a few more murders to his record in the next week or two. Maybe even kill himself.'

'This isn't any nut,' Hoval insisted. 'It's one of your political cases. He won't kill anyone else — not until he gets a chance to set up another cop.'

'You're wrong about him,' the technician said.

Hoval shook his head, took a long drink of his lemon blend. 'You bleeding-heart liberals astound me. Can't stop looking for simple answers.'

The waitress brought the pale man's coffee.

When she went away, he said, 'I haven't noticed any blood on my shirt in the vicinity of my heart. And I am not a political liberal. And I think *your* answer is more simplistic than mine.'

'The country's going to hell in a handbasket, and you're blaming it all on psychotics and fruitcakes.'

'Well,' the technician said, finally putting down the salt shaker, 'I almost hope you're right. Because if this guy *is* a nut, and if he *is* loose another week or two . . .'

Friday

Eighteen

By two o'clock Friday morning, sixteen hours after they had left Denver, Alex felt as if he belonged in a hospital ward for terminally ill patients. His legs were cramped and heavy. His buttocks pinched and burned as if they were jammed full of needles, and his back ached all the way from the base of his spine to the back of his skull. And these were only the first in a long list of complaints: he was sweat-damp, rumpled, and unclean from having missed last night's shower; his eyes were bloodshot, grainy, and sore; the crisp black stubble of his one-day beard itched badly; his mouth was fuzzy and dry and tasted like sour milk; his arms ached dully from holding the damned steering wheel for hour after hour, mile after mile . . .

'You awake?' he asked Colin. In the darkness, with the gentle country music coming out of the radio, the boy should have been asleep.

'I'm here,' Colin said.

'Should try to catch a few winks.'

'I'm afraid the car is going to break down,' Colin said. 'I can't sleep for worrying about it.'

'The car's okay,' Doyle said. 'The body got dented in a little, but that's all. The only reason it begins to shake when we go past eighty-five is that the wheel starts brushing against the indented metal.'

'I'll still worry,' Colin said.

'We'll stop at the next likely place and freshen up,' Doyle said. 'We both need it. And the car's low on gas.'

Late Thursday afternoon they had headed southwest across Utah on a series of back-roads, then picked up the secondary two-lane Route 21, which carried them northwest again. The swift desert sunset came, faded rapidly from a fiery orange-red to solemn purple and then a deep and velvety black. And still they drove, crossing into Nevada and switching over to Route 50, which they intended to follow from one end of the Silver state clear to the other.

Shortly after ten o'clock they stopped to get gasoline and to call Courtney from a pay phone. They pretended that they were at their motel, because Alex could not see any good reason to worry her now. Though they *had* been through a harrowing ordeal, it was probably all finished now. They had lost their stalker. There was no need to alarm her unnecessarily. They could give her the full story when they finally got to San Francisco.

From ten-thirty Thursday night until two o'clock Friday morning, they passed through what had once been the heart of the romantic Old West. The forbidding sand plains lay dark and empty to the left and right. Hard, barren mountains thrust up without warning and fell sharply away, out of place even if they had spent millennia here. Cactus loomed at both sides of the road, and rabbits occasionally fled across the pavement in the yellow glare of their headlights. If the trip had gone differently, if there had been no madman on their tail for the last two thousand miles, perhaps Nevada would have been a pleasure, a chance to indulge in nostalgia and a few of Colin's games. But now it was a bore, just something to be passed through before they could get to San Francisco.

At two-thirty they stopped at a combination service station and all-night diner. While the Thunderbird was topped off with gas and oil, Colin used the bathroom, freshened up for the next long leg of the marathon drive. In the diner, they ordered hamburgers and French fries. And while those were sizzling, Alex went into the men's room to shave and wash his face.

And to take two caffeine tablets.

He had bought a packet of them earlier in the night, at the service station where they had stopped just before leaving Utah. Colin had been in the car at the time and had not witnessed the purchase. Alex did not want the boy to know about the tablets. Colin was already much too tense for his own good. It would not be good for him to find out that Doyle, despite all his assurances, was getting sleepy at the wheel.

He looked at his reflection in the cracked mirror above the dirty washbasin, grimaced. 'You look terrible.'

The reflection remained mute.

They by-passed the exit to Reno and stayed on

Route 50 until they found a motel just east of Carson City. It was a shabby place, decaying at the edges. But neither of them had the energy to look any further. The dashboard clock read eight-thirty – more than twenty-two hours since they had left Denver.

In their room, Colin went straight for his bed and flopped down. 'Wake me in six months,' he said.

Alex went into the bath and closed the door. He used his electric razor to touch up the shave he had taken six hours before, brushed his teeth, took a hot shower. When he came back into the main room, Colin was asleep; the boy had not even bothered to undress. Doyle put on clean clothes, then woke him.

'What's the matter?' the boy asked, nearly leaping off the bed when Doyle touched his shoulder.

'You can't sleep yet.'

'Why not?' Colin rubbed at his face.

'I'm going out. I won't leave you alone, so I guess you'll have to come with me.'

'Out? Where?'

Alex hesitated a moment. 'To . . . To buy a gun.'

Now Colin was wide awake. He stood up and straightened his Phantom of the Opera shirt. 'Do you really think we need a gun? Do you think that man in the Automover—'

'He probably won't show up again.'

'Then—'

'I only said he *probably* won't. But I just don't know any more . . . I've thought about it all night, all the way across Nevada, and I can't be sure of anything.' He wiped at his own face, pulling off his weariness. 'And then when I'm pretty sure that we've lost him – well, I think about some of the people we've run into. That service station attendant near Harrisburg. The woman at the Lazy Time Motel. I think about Captain Ackridge . . . I don't know. It's not that I think those people are dangerous. It's just that they represent something that's happening . . . Well, it seems to me we ought to have a gun, more to keep it in the house in San Francisco than to protect us for the last few hours of this trip.'

'Then why not buy it in San Francisco?'

'I think I'll sleep better if we get it now,' Alex said.

'But I thought you were a pacifist?'

'I am.'

Colin shook his head. 'A pacifist who carries a gun?'

'Stranger things happen every day,' Doyle said.

A few minutes past eleven o'clock, an hour and a half after they had gone out, Doyle and the boy returned to the motel room. Alex closed the door, shutting out the insufferable desert heat. He twisted the dead lock and put the guard chain in place. He tried the knob, but it would not turn.

Colin took the small, heavy pasteboard box to the bed and sat down with it. He lifted the lid and looked inside at the .32-calibre pistol and the box of ammunition. He had stayed in the car when Doyle went to buy it, and he had not been allowed to open the box on the short ride back. This was his first look at the weapon. He made a sour face.

'You said the man in the sporting-goods store called it a *lady*'s gun.'

'That's right,' Doyle said, sitting down on the edge of his bed and taking off his boots. He knew he was not going to be able to stay awake more than another minute or two.

'Why did he say that?'

'Compared to a .45, it has less punch, less kick, and makes a great deal less noise. It's the kind of pistol a woman usually buys.'

'Did you have any trouble buying it, since you're from out of state and all?'

Doyle stretched out on the bed. 'No. In fact, it was too damned easy.'

Nineteen

Friday afternoon, George Leland drove across the Nevada badlands towards Reno, his eyes brimming with pain even though the sunglasses he wore cut out half the glare from the white-white sand. He did not make good time. He was unable to keep his mind on his driving.

Since that especially severe headache he had suffered early Thursday morning when he had gone after Alex Doyle with a garden axe, Leland had found his thoughts wandering freely, almost beyond his control. He was not able to concentrate on anything for more than five minutes at a stretch. His mind jumped from subject to subject like a motion picture full of quick-cuts.

Time and again he snapped from a daydream, surprised to find himself behind the wheel of the van. He had driven miles and miles while his mind was elsewhere . . . Apparently some fraction of his attention *was* on the road ahead and the traffic around him; but it was a very *small* fraction. If he had been on a heavily used freeway instead of out here on the flat, open wastelands, he would have killed himself, would have demolished the van during one of those daydreams.

Courtney was always there with him, in and out of the dreams. Now, as he came back again to the sand-flanked highway and the reality of the Chevrolet grumbling crankily beneath him, she was perched only a couple of feet away, her long legs drawn up on the seat beneath her.

'I almost had them yesterday,' Leland said contritely. 'But those damn worn tyres . . .'

'That's okay, George,' she said, close yet far-away.

'No, Courtney. I should have nailed them. And . . . Last night, when I checked the motel in Salt Lake City, *they were not there*.' He was puzzled by that. 'In that book of his, it said they'd stay at the Highlands Motel in Salt Lake City. What happened to them?'

She must not have known, for she did not answer.

Leland wiped his left hand on his trousers while he held the wheel in his right, repeated the gesture and drove with the left. 'I looked in all the motels near the Highlands. They weren't staying in any of them. I've lost them. Somehow, they got away from me.'

'You'll pick them up again,' she said. He had hoped that she would be sympathetic and would encourage him. Lovely Courtney. You could always depend on Courtney.

'Maybe I will,' he said, squinting out at the rolling hills of sand and the distant blue-and-rose mountains. 'But how? And where?' He hoped she had the answer to that.

She did. 'In San Francisco, of course.'

'San Francisco?'

'You have my address there,' Courtney said. 'And that's where they're going. Isn't it?'

'Yes,' he said. 'It sure is.'

'There you are.'

'But . . . Maybe I can catch them in Reno tonight.'

The lovely, soft-voiced, ethereal girl said, 'They'll change motels again. You won't find them.'

He nodded. It was true.

For a while, then, he went away from her. He was not in Nevada now, but in Philadelphia. Three months ago. He had gone downtown to see a film which had been entertaining and which . . . Well, the girl in it had looked so much like Courtney that he had been unable to sleep that night. He saw the film the next night too, and he learned from the lobby posters that the actress who fascinated him was Carol Lynley. But he soon forgot that. He went back to the film night after night, and she became the *real* Courtney. She was perfect. Long yellow-white hair, elfin features, those eyes that seemed to pierce him . . . Gradually, the sixth and seventh and eighth and ninth times he saw the movie, he began to experience a regeneration of sexual desire – which was odd, because the film was family fare. Finally, though, he had gone bar-hopping and had picked up a girl. He had made it with her . . . But she looked nothing like Courtney. Afterward, when he was spent, lying atop her, he looked into her face and saw that she was not Courtney, and he was angry. He felt that he had been tricked. She had cheated him. And so he started hitting her, slamming his hard fist into her face, over and over until—

He blinked at the blue sky, white sand, grey-black road. 'Well,' he said to the girl on the seat beside him, 'I guess I will skip Reno. They won't stay in the right motel, anyway. I'll just go right on in to Frisco.'

The golden girl smiled.

'Right on in to Frisco,' Leland said. 'They won't expect me there. They won't be ready for anything. I can take care of them real easy. And then we can be together. Can't we?'

'Yes,' she said, just as he wanted her to say.

'We'd be happy again, wouldn't we?'

'Yes.'

'You'd let me touch you again.'

'Yes, George.'

'Let me sleep with you again.'

'Yes.'

'Live with me?'

'Yes.'

'And people would stop being nasty to me.'

'Yes.'

'You don't have to worry about me hurting you, Courtney,' he said. 'When you first left me, I wanted to hurt you. I wanted to kill you. But not any more. We're going to be together again, and I wouldn't hurt you for the world.'

Twenty

Courtney answered the telephone on the first ring, and she was even more exuberant than usual. 'I've been waiting for your call,' she said. 'I've got some good news.'

Alex was ready for a piece of good news, especially if it was delivered in that warm, throaty voice of hers. 'What is it?'

'I got the job, Alex!'

'At the magazine?'

'Yes!' She laughed into the phone, and he could almost see her standing there with her golden head thrown back and her taut throat exposed. 'Isn't it wonderful?'

Her happiness almost made up for everything that had gone wrong in the last few days. 'You're absolutely sure it's what you wanted?'

'It's better than what I wanted.'

'So . . . You and Colin will be old San Franciscans in short order – and I'll have to take a month off just to catch up with you.'

'You know what the pay is?'

'Ten dollars a week?' he asked.

'Be serious.'

'Fifteen?'

'Eighty-five hundred a year. To start.'

He whistled. 'Not bad for your first really professional job. But look, you aren't the only one with good news.'

'Oh?'

Doyle looked at Colin, who was squeezed into the telephone booth with him, and he tried not to sound like a liar when he told the lie: 'We got into Reno a few minutes ago.' In fact, they had never gone to Reno at all, but to Carson City. And they had arrived early this morning, not minutes ago. They had slept all afternoon, right through the supper hour, and had awakened at half past eight, little more than an hour ago. 'Neither one of us is sleepy.' This was true enough, though he did not want to have to explain *why* neither one of them was sleepy, since they were not supposed to have been dozing in a motel all day. 'It's about two hundred and fifty miles to San Francisco, so . . .'

'You're coming home tonight?' she asked.

'We thought we might as well.'

'Look, if you're sleepy – sleep.'

'We aren't sleepy.'

'One day doesn't matter,' she said. 'Don't get in a big rush to finish the trip. If you fall asleep at the wheel—'

'You'll lose a new Thunderbird but gain valuable insurance money,' he finished for her.

'That isn't funny.'

'No. I guess it isn't. I'm sorry.' He was irritable, he knew, only because he did not like to lie to her. He felt cheap and somehow dirty, even though he was only lying to save her unnecessary worry.

'You're *sure* you feel up to it?'

'Yes, Courtney.'

'Then I'll keep the bed warm.'

'*That* I might not feel up to.'

'You will,' she said. She laughed again, more softly this time. 'You always are *up* to it.'

'Bad joke,' he said. 'Bad joke.'

'But one of those that just had to be made. So . . . What time can I expect you and the Marvellous Mite?'

Doyle looked at his wristwatch. 'It's a quarter to ten now. Give us forty-five minutes for supper . . . We should get to the house around three in the morning, if we don't get *too* lost.'

She gave him a moist kiss via telephone. 'Until three, darling.'

At eleven o'clock George Leland passed a sign which gave the mileage to San Francisco. He looked down at the speedometer and did some figuring. He was not as quick about it as he once would have been. The numbers were slippery. He could not seem to add with even a third-grader's skill. And he was not as sure of himself as he had once been, either, for he had to refigure the thing three times before he was satisfied with the answer.

He looked at the shimmering golden girl beside him. 'We'll reach your place by one o'clock. Maybe one-thirty,' he said.

213

Saturday

Twenty-one

Courtney gathered up the stacks of rubbish that had accumulated from moving and taking delivery on new furniture – empty wooden packing crates, cardboard boxes, mounds of shredded newspapers, plastic and paper wrappings, wire, cord, rope – and put it all in the guest bedroom, which had not yet been furnished. It made quite a large, unsightly hill of rubble in the centre of the carpet. She stepped into the hall and closed the door on the junk. There. Now they wouldn't have to look at it or think about it until Monday, when it would become necessary to haul the whole lot away somewhere to make room for the guest-room furniture. It was a bit like sweeping dirt under a carpet, she supposed. But as long as no one lifted up the carpet to look, what was wrong with that?

She went back to their bedroom and stood in the doorway, surveying it. The dresser, highboy, nightstands and bed were all of matching heavy, dark wood which looked as if it had been hand-carved and hand-polished. The carpet was a deep-blue shag. The bedspread and curtains were a rich dark-gold velvet that looked almost as soft and honied as her own skin when she had a good tan. All in all, she thought, it was a damned sexy room.

Of course, the spread didn't hang perfectly even all around. And there was a cluster of perfume and make-up bottles on the dresser. And maybe the full-length mirror needed polishing . . . But all these things were what made it a Courtney Doyle Room. She left her mark of casual, minimal, harmless disarray wherever she lived.

'Remember,' she had warned Alex on the night before their wedding, 'you aren't getting a good housekeeper.'

'I don't *want* to marry a housekeeper,' he had said. 'Hell, I can *hire* housekeepers by the dozen.'

'And I'm not a really terrific cook.'

'Why did God make restaurants?' he asked.

'And,' she had said, scowling at the thought of her own sloppiness and slothfulness, 'I usually let the laundry pile up until I either have to do the wash or buy all new clothes.'

'Courtney, what do you think God made the *Chinese* for, if not to do laundry? Huh?'

Remembering that exchange, how they had broken into fits of laughter and giggled helplessly, holding each other and rocking on the floor like silly children, she smiled and went over to their new bed and sat down on it, testing the springs.

She actually had tested them before. She had stripped off all her clothes and jumped up and down in the centre of the mattress, just as she had told Alex on the telephone. It had seemed a splendid idea at the time. But the exercise and the cool air on her bare skin had given her ideas and an appetite for loving. She could hardly get to sleep that night for wanting him. She kept thinking of Alex, of what it was like with him, kept thinking how perfect they were together and how bedtime with him was unlike anything she had ever known with anyone else.

They were good together in many ways, not just in bed. They liked the same books, the same movies, and usually the same people. If it was true that opposites attract, then duplicates attract even more.

'Do you think we'll ever get bored with each other?' she had asked him towards the end of the first week of their honeymoon.

'Bored?' he had asked, faking an enormous yawn.

'Seriously.'

'We won't be bored for a minute,' he said.

'But we're so similar, so—'

'Only three kinds of people bore me,' he had said. 'First: someone who can only talk about himself. And you're not an egomaniac.'

'Second?'

'Someone who can't talk about *anything*. That kind bores me to tears. But you are an intelligent, active, exciting woman who always has something going. You'll never be without something to say.'

'Third?'

'The most boring person of all is the one who doesn't listen when I talk about myself,' Alex said, half serious but trying to get a laugh out of her as well.

'I always listen,' she said. 'I like to hear you talk

about yourself. You are a fascinating subject.'

Now, sitting on the bed which they would share tonight, she realized that *listening* to each other was the main thing that made their relationship work so well. She wanted to *know* him, and he wanted to fully understand her. He wanted to know what she was thinking and doing, and she wanted to be a part of all that concerned him. When you got right down to it, maybe they were not duplicates at all. Maybe, because they listened so well, they came to understand and appreciate each other's tastes and, soon, to share them. They did not duplicate each other so much as they helped each other expand and grow.

The future seemed so promising, and she was so happy that she hugged herself, an unconscious expression of satisfaction and delight which she had unknowingly passed on to Colin.

Downstairs, the doorbell rang.

She looked at the bedside clock: ten minutes past two.

Could they be here an hour early? Could he have overestimated the length of the drive by that much?

She got off the bed and hurried into the hall, took the stairs two at a time. She was excited at the prospect of seeing them and asking lots of questions about their trip, but . . . At the same time she was a bit angry. Had he just mistaken the length of time they would need to drive in from Reno? Or had he broken all the speed limits getting here. If he did . . . How dare he risk their future only to shave an hour off a five-day trip? By the time she reached the front door, she was almost as angry as she was pleased to know they were finally home.

She pulled off the chain and opened the door.

'Hello, Courtney,' he said, reaching out to gently touch her face.

'George? What are you doing here?'

Twenty-two

Before she could turn and run, before she could even grasp that there was something sinister about his unexpected appearance, he took her arm in a vicelike grip and walked her over to the gold-and-red Spanish sofa, sat down with her. He looked around the room and nodded, smiled. 'It's nice. I'll like it here.'

'George? What—'

Still gripping her arm in one hand, he touched her face, traced the delicate line of her jaw. 'You're so lovely,' he said.

'George, why are you here?' She was somewhat afraid, though not quite terrified. His appearance did not make any sense, but it was no reason for her to go to pieces.

He let his hand slide along her throat, felt her pulse with his finger tips, then dropped the hand and cupped one of her heavy unrestrained breasts. 'Just as lovely as ever,' he said.

'Please, Don't touch me like that,' she said. She tried to pull away from him.

He held her tightly, and his free hand followed her. He caressed the other breast now. 'You said that you'd let me touch you again.'

'What do you mean?' His fingers were digging

into her arm so deeply that shooting pains exploded in her shoulder.

'You said I could make love to you again.' His voice was low and dreamy. 'Like before.'

'No. I never said that.'

'Yes, Courtney. You did.'

She looked into his dark-ringed, bloodshot eyes, into the vaguely unfocused blue circles, and for the first time in her life she experienced the fear which belonged solely to women. She knew he might try to rape her. And she knew that even as gaunt as he was, he would be strong enough to do it . . . But wasn't it ridiculous to fear him this way? Hadn't she been to bed with him dozens of times in the past, before he had started to change? What was there to fear, then? But she knew. It was not the sex that she feared. It was the force involved, the violent potential, the humiliation and the sense of being *used*. She did not know how he had got here or how he had learned their address. She did not know his circumstances or full intentions. But none of that mattered worth a damn. All that mattered right now was whether or not he would rape her. She felt weak, helpless, and oppressed. She was cold and hollow inside, trembling at the prospect of having to accept his forced attentions.

'You better not stay here any longer,' she said, despising herself for the tremor in her voice. 'Alex will be here in a few minutes.'

Leland smiled. 'Well, of course he will. I *know* that.'

She could not figure out what he wanted, what he thought he could achieve beyond the brief, vicious taking of her. 'Then why are you here?'

'We talked about that before.'

'No. No, we did not.'

'Sure, Courtney. You remember. In the van, we talked. On the way here. You and me. We've talked about it for several days now – how we could take care of them and then be together again.'

She was no longer merely frightened. She was terrified. Finally he had gone over the edge. Whatever was wrong with him – some physical illness or a psychological disease – it had at last pushed him beyond sanity. 'George, you've got to listen. Are you listening to me?'

'Sure, Courtney. I like your voice.'

She shuddered involuntarily. 'George, you're not well. Whatever has been wrong with you for the past two years—'

The smile faded from his face as he interrupted her. 'I'm perfectly healthy. Why do you always insist I'm not?'

'Did you ever have those X-rays that the doctor—'

'Shut up!' he said. 'I don't want to talk about it.'

'George, if you're sick, maybe there's still something—'

She saw the blow coming, but she could not pull away from it in time. His big calloused hand struck her hard alongside the head. Her teeth rattled. She thought that was an almost funny sound . . .

But then the darkness rushed up at her, and she knew that she was going to faint. Unconscious, she would be even more helpless. And she realized, suddenly, that rape might be the least of her worries. He might not rape her at all. He might kill her.

She cried out, or thought that she did, and then she fell away into an inky pool.

Leland went out to the van and got the .32-calibre pistol which he had forgotten to bring with him the first time. He came back into the living room and stood by the sofa, looking down at her, admiring her golden hair and her freckles, the exquisite lines of her face.

Why couldn't she have been nice to him? All the way across the country, she had been nice. When he told her to stop nagging him about something, she had stopped at once. But now she was the bitch again, picking at him, trying to say his mind was going on him. Didn't she know that was impossible? It was his mind that had gotten him all the scholarships, years ago. It was his superb mind which had gotten him off that damn farm, away from the poverty and the Bible-thumping and his father's paddle. So he *couldn't* be losing his mind. She only said that to frighten him.

He put the pistol barrel in her ear.

But he could not pull the trigger.

'I love you,' he told her, although she could not hear him. He sat down on the floor beside the couch, and he started to cry.

He snapped back from a daydream and realized that he was undressing her. While his thoughts had been elsewhere, he had pulled off her thin blue sweater, and now he was fumbling at the catch of her jeans. He stopped what he was doing and looked at her. Naked to the waist, she looked like a little girl despite the firm lines of her breasts. She seemed defenceless and weak and in need of protection.

This was not the way.

Leland knew, suddenly, that if he just tied her up and put her on ice until he had dealt with Doyle and the boy, she would be all right. When they were dead, she would realize that Leland was all she had. And then they could be together.

Lifting her as easily as he would have an infant, he carried her upstairs and put her on the bed in the master bedroom. He retrieved her sweater from the living-room floor and somehow slipped it onto her again.

Fifteen minutes later he had tied her hands and feet with rope that he found on the junk heap in the guest bedroom, and he had used a length of adhesive tape to seal her mouth.

He was sitting on the bed beside her, staring into her eyes, when they fluttered open and found him.

'Don't be afraid,' he said.

She cried out behind the gag.

'I won't hurt you,' he said. 'I love you.' He touched her long, fine hair. 'In a little while everything will be okay. We'll be happy together, because we won't have anyone else in the world but each other.'

Twenty-three

'This is our street?' Colin asked as the Thunderbird laboured up the steep lane towards a cluster
of lights near the top.

'That's right.'

Beyond the aisle of well-shaped cherry trees,
the darkness of Lincoln Park lay on their left. To
the right, the land shelved down through more
darkness to the city's lights and the shimmering
necklace of the harbour and the bay bridge. It was
a stunning sight, even at three o'clock in the
morning.

'This is *some* place,' the boy said.

'You like it, huh?'

'It beats Philadelphia.'

Doyle laughed. 'It sure does.'

'That's our house up there?' Colin asked, pointing towards the only lights ahead of them.

'Yes. And almost three whole acres of land
around it.' Coming home to the place for the first
time now, he knew that it was worth every penny
they had paid for it, though the price had initially
seemed exorbitant. He thought of Courtney there,
waiting. He remembered the tree outside the
bedroom window, and he wondered if they
would keep each other awake until dawn, when

they could see the morning sun slanting down on the blue bay . . .

'I hope Courtney isn't too mad about the lies we told her,' Colin said, still looking out across the edge of the city towards the dark ocean. 'If she was, it would spoil this.'

'She won't be angry,' Doyle said, knowing that she would be, just a little and for just a few minutes. 'She'll be glad we're safe and sound.'

The house lights were close now, though the outline of the structure was hidden by a wall of deeply shadowed trees that rose behind it.

Doyle slowed down, looking for the entrance to the driveway. He found it and turned in. Thousands of small oval stones crunched under the tyres.

He had to drive clear around to the side of the house before he saw the Chevrolet van parked by the garage.

Twenty-four

Doyle got out of the damaged car on the passenger's side, put one hand on Colin's thin shoulder. 'You get back in there,' he said. 'Stay here. If you see anyone but me come out of the house, leave the car and run to the neighbours. The nearest ones are downhill.'

'Shouldn't we call the cops and—'

'There isn't time for that. He's inside with Courtney.' Alex felt his stomach twist, and he thought he was going to vomit. A bitter fluid touched the back of his throat, but he choked it down.

'Another couple of minutes—'

'Might make all the difference.'

Doyle turned away from the Thunderbird and hurried across the dark lawn towards the front door, which was ajar.

How was it possible? Who was this man who could follow them wherever they went, who could catch up with them no matter how much they changed their plans? Who in the hell was he that he could drive ahead and wait for them here? He seemed more than maniacal. He was almost superhuman, satanic.

And what had he done to Courtney? If he had

hurt her in any way . . . Alex was caught up between rage and terror. It was frightening to realize that even when you had the courage to face up to violence, you could not protect those you loved. More than that, you couldn't know where the danger would come from or in what form.

He reached the front door, pushed it open, and stepped into the house before he thought that he might have walked into a trap. Suddenly he remembered all too clearly the cunning and ferocity which the madman had shown when he had been swinging that axe . . .

Doyle crouched against the wall, sheltering behind a telephone stand, making as small a target of himself as he could. He looked quickly around the front room.

It was deserted.

All the lights were blazing, but no madman was here. And no Courtney.

The house was very quiet.

Too quiet?

Keeping his back to the wall, he went from the living room to the dining room, the shag carpet absorbing the noise of each footstep. But the dining room was also empty.

In the kitchen, three plates, knives, forks, and spoons had been laid out on the butcher-block table along with various other utensils. She had planned a late-night snack for them.

Doyle's heart was pounding painfully. His breathing was so harsh and deep that he felt certain it could be heard from one end of the house to the other.

He kept thinking: Courtney, Courtney, Courtney . . .

The sunken den and the screened-in back porch were also deserted. Everything was neat and orderly – or, rather, as neat and orderly as things could be in Courtney's house. And that must be a good sign. Right? No traces of a struggle, no overturned furniture, no blood . . .

'Courtney!'

He had intended to remain silent. But now it seemed terribly important to call her name, as if the spoken word were a magic charm that would heal whatever the madman had done to her.

'Courtney!'

No reply.

'Courtney, where are you?'

In the back of his mind, Doyle knew that he should calm down. He should shut up for a minute and rethink the situation, consider his options once more before making another move. He was not going to help either Courtney or Colin if he acted stupidly, precipitously, and got himself killed.

However, with the silent house pressing in on him, he was temporarily incapable of rational behaviour.

'Courtney!'

Bent forward like a soldier landing on an enemy-held beach, he ran up the main stairs two at a time. At the top, he grabbed the head of the banister to keep his balance, and he gasped for breath.

Along the second-floor hallway, all the doors were closed, each like the lid of a surprise package.

The guest bedroom was the nearest. He took three steps across the hall and threw that door open.

For a moment he could not understand what he was seeing. Boards, boxes, papers, and other junk were stacked in the middle of the room, a pile of rubble in the centre of the nice new carpet. He took several steps forward, past the threshold, curiously disquieted by the incongruity of what lay there.

The thick, slow voice came from the doorway immediately behind him. 'You took her away from me.'

Alex made himself fall to the left as he turned. But it was hopeless. In spite of that manoeuvre, the bullet slammed into him and knocked him all the way down.

The tall, broad-shouldered man stood in the doorway, smiling. He held a pistol quite like the one which Doyle had bought in Carson City – and had thoughtlessly left in the car when he needed it most.

He thought: It just proves that you can't turn a pacifist into a violent man overnight. You can pump him up with courage, but you can't make him think in terms of guns . . .

It was a ridiculous thing to be running through his mind just then. Therefore, he stopped thinking about it and gave himself up to the ruby-coloured darkness.

When George Leland came back from the daydream about the farm and his father, he was sitting on the edge of Courtney's bed. He was caressing her face with one hand.

Her body was as stiff as a plaster statue as she strained against her bonds. She was trying to say something behind the adhesive tape, and she had begun to weep.

'It's okay,' Leland said. 'I took care of him.'

She tossed back and forth, trying to shake off his hand.

Leland looked at the pistol in his other hand, and he realized that he had only shot Doyle once. Maybe the sonofabitch was not dead. He ought to go back and make sure.

But he did not want to leave Courtney. He wanted to touch her some more, maybe even make love to her. Feel her soft, warm skin gliding over the calloused pads of his fingers. Enjoy her. Enjoy being with her. The two of them together again . . . He spread his hands on her chest and pressed down with enough force to make her be still. He petted her face and sifted her golden hair through his fingers.

For the moment he had all but forgotten Alex Doyle.

He did not think of Colin at all.

The boy heard the shot. It was muffled by the walls of the house, but it was instantly identifiable.

He opened the door and jumped out of the car. He ran halfway down the drive, then stopped when he suddenly realized that he had nowhere to go.

Downhill, the houses remained dark, as did those uphill. Apparently no one had been awakened by the shot.

Okay. But he could still go wake them up and tell them what had happened, couldn't he? Even as he considered that, he knew it was useless. He thought of the way Captain Ackridge had treated Alex. And while he knew that the neighbours would be friendly, he also knew that they would not believe him – at least not in time to help Alex and Courtney. An eleven-year-old boy? He would be humoured, perhaps scolded. But never believed.

He turned and ran back to the car, stopped at the open door and looked at the house. No one had come outside.

Get on with it, he thought. Alex wouldn't hesitate. He went right in after Courtney, didn't he? You want to be an adult or a frightened child?

He sat on the edge of the car seat and opened the glove compartment, took out the small pasteboard box. He lifted out the pistol and put it on the seat, fumbled for ammunition. In his eleven years he had never handled a gun before, but he thought the loading procedure looked pretty elementary. The safety was marked by tiny letters which he could just make out in the dim overhead light: SAFETY ON OFF. He pushed it to OFF.

Twenty-five

Alex stared at the broken crates, shredded newspapers, and other garbage for a minute or two before he realized where he was and remembered what had happened. The madman, with a gun this time . . .

'Courtney?' he asked softly.

When he moved, he triggered the pain. It came in waves and made him feel old and weak. He had been hit high in the left shoulder blade, and he felt as if someone had liberally salted the wound.

Missed the heart, at least, he thought. Must have missed everything vital. But that was only slightly comforting.

He got one hand under himself and pushed up to his knees, dripping blood on the carpet under him. The pain increased; the waves crashed through him with greater force and more speed.

He kept expecting to hear another shot and to be knocked forward into the boxes and newspapers. But he climbed laboriously to his feet and turned around to find the doorway empty, the madman gone.

Clutching his shoulder with his good hand, blood bubbling between his fingers, he started across the room. He was halfway to the hall door when he thought it would be a good idea to have some sort of weapon before he went looking for the man. But what? He turned around again and looked at the stack of junk, saw just what he needed. He went back and picked up a four-foot-long, three-inch-wide board from a broken wooden packing crate. Three long bent nails protruded from one side of it. It would do. Again he turned towards the doorway and crossed the room.

Those eight steps seemed more like eight hundred. By the time he had taken them, he needed to stop and rest. His chest was tight, and his breath did not come easily. He leaned against the wall just inside the door, out of sight of anyone in the second-floor hallway.

You've got to do better than this, he told himself, closing his eyes to block out the dizzying movement of the room. Even if you do find him, you won't be able to stop him from doing whatever he pleases to Courtney and Colin. You *can't* be this weak. It's shock. You were shot. You're bleeding. And you're suffering from shock. Anyone would be. But you have to overcome it soon, or you might as well sit down and bleed to death.

Leland pulled the tape off her mouth and touched her bloodless lips. 'It's all right now, Courtney. Doyle is dead. We don't have to worry about him. It's just you and me against everyone.'

She was unable to speak. She was no longer the golden girl, but was as pale as milk.

'I'm going to let you up now,' he said, smiling.

'If you're good, that is. If you behave yourself, I'll untie your feet and hands – so that we can make love. Would you like that?'

She shook her head no.

'Sure you would.'

On the first level, towards the back of the house, a window broke and crashed across the bare floor.

'It's the police,' she said, not knowing for sure who it was, wanting to frighten him.

He stood up without untying her. 'No,' he said. 'It's the boy. How could I have forgotten the boy?' Perplexed, he turned away from the bed and started for the door.

'Don't hurt him!' she cried. 'For God's sake, leave him alone!'

Leland did not hear her. He was able to fully perceive and think about only one thing at a time. Right now, that was the boy. He had to find the boy and kill him, eliminate this last obstacle between himself and Courtney.

He left the master bedroom, went down the hall to the stairs.

When Alex heard the glass shattering downstairs, he thought that Colin must have brought help. But then he remembered that the front door was standing open. Why would anyone not use it?

He knew, at once, that Colin had not gone for help. Instead, the boy had taken the pistol from the glove compartment, the pistol Doyle had not remembered at the right time. Colin had distrusted the open front door and had gone around to the back of the house to find a way in. He was coming to the rescue all by himself. It was a very brave thing to do. It would also get him killed.

Doyle pushed away from the wall just as Courtney screamed, and he nearly tripped over his own feet in surprise. She was alive! Of course, he had been telling himself that she would be okay – but he had not believed it. He had expected to find a corpse.

He turned towards the door to the hall just in time to see the madman reach the top of the stairs and start down.

In the master bedroom down the hall, Courtney screamed again. 'Don't hurt him! Don't kill my brother too!'

Too? Then she believes that I'm already dead, Doyle thought.

'Courtney!' He did not care if the man downstairs heard him. 'I'm okay. Colin will be okay.'

'Alex? Is that *you*?'

'It's me,' he said. Holding the crude weapon tightly in his good hand, he went across the landing and down the steps, hurrying after the madman.

Twenty-six

Colin tried the kitchen door. It was locked. He did not want to waste time trying all the windows, and he was not about to walk through the front entrance which had so completely swallowed Alex. He hesitated only a second, then reversed the pistol, held it by the barrel, and used the butt to smash in one of the large panes of glass in the door.

He thought he ought to be able to get inside quickly enough to find a good hiding place before the madman reached the kitchen. Then he would come out of concealment and shoot the man in the back.

But he could not find the latch. He thrust one arm through the empty windowpane, scratching it on the remaining shards of glass, and he felt around on the inside of the door. But the lock mechanism escaped his fingers. There did not seem to *be* a lock switch.

He looked at the other end of the well-lighted kitchen, at the door the man would come through.

Precious seconds passed while he fumbled noisily, desperately, for the unseen latch.

And suddenly, he found it. He cried out, twisted it, and pushed the door open, stumbling into the kitchen with the .32 held out in front of him.

Before he could look for a place to hide, George Leland came through the other door. Colin recognized the man at once, though he had not seen him in two years. But the recognition did not freeze him. He pointed the gun at Leland's chest and pulled the trigger.

The recoil numbed his arms clear up to the elbows.

Leland moved in like an express train, roaring wordlessly. He swung one open hand and sent the boy sprawling on the shiny tile floor.

Colin's pistol clattered among the table and chair legs, out of reach. And the boy knew, as he watched the gun spin away, that his first and only shot had missed the mark.

Alex was halfway through the dining room, closing in on the stranger's unprotected back while the man was still unaware of him, when the shot exploded in the kitchen. He heard the madman shout, saw him leap forward. He heard Colin squeal and something overturn an instant later.

But he did not know who had shot whom.

Running the last few feet into the kitchen, he raised the spiked board over his head.

On the floor by the refrigerator, Colin was trying to get to his feet. Two yards away, the stranger raised his pistol . . .

Crying out in terror and a sort of savage glee, Alex brought his club down, swung it with all his strength. The three spikes raked the back of the other man's skull.

The stranger howled, dropped the gun, grabbed at his head with both hands. He staggered two steps and was brought up by the heavy butcher-block table.

Alex struck again. The spikes pierced the man's hands this time, briefly nailing them to his skull before Doyle jerked the board away.

The madman came around to face his attacker, his bleeding hands thrown up to ward off the next blow.

Alex met the wide blue eyes, and he thought that there was definitely more than a trace of sanity in them now, something clean and rational. The madness had temporarily fallen away.

Alex did not care about that. He swung the club again. The spikes grazed the stranger's face, furrowed the flesh, drew three red streaks across one cheek.

'Please,' the man said, leaning back over the table, crossing his arms in front of his face. 'Please! Please stop!'

But Doyle knew that if he stopped now, the insanity might well return to those eyes quickly and with a vengeance. The big man might lurch forward and regain the advantage. And then *he* would show no mercy.

Doyle thought of what the sonofabitch might have done to Courtney, what he would have done to Colin. He struck again. And again. He struck harder and faster each time, ripping the nails into the man's arms, neck, the sides of his skull . . .

Doyle whimpered, painfully aware that he was now the maniac and that the man on the table had become the right man. But he went on anyway, slashing and tearing with all his strength.

The stranger fell to the floor and cracked his head on the tiles. He looked sadly up at Doyle and tried to say something. Blood ran from a hundred cuts and, suddenly, it poured out of his nose like water from a set of faucets. He died.

For a full minute Alex stood over the corpse, staring down at his handiwork. He was numb. He felt nothing: not anger, shame, pity, sorrow, not anything at all. It did not seem right to have killed a man and feel no remorse.

Waves of pain spread out again from his wounded shoulder. He realized that he had been using both hands to hold the club, that he had put both of his shoulders into each brutal swing of it. He dropped the board on top of the corpse and turned away from both of them.

Colin was standing in the corner by the refrigerator. He was sheet-white and trembling. He looked smaller and skinnier than ever.

'Are you okay?' Doyle asked.

The boy looked at him, unable to speak.

'Colin.'

The boy only shook.

Doyle took a step towards him.

Suddenly crying out, Colin ran forward, flung himself against Doyle, hugged the man around the waist. He was sobbing hysterically. He looked up, eyes glistening behind the thick glasses, and said, 'You won't ever leave us, will you?'

'Leave you? Of course not,' Doyle said. He grabbed the boy under the arms, lifted him up and held him tightly.

'Say you won't leave us!' Colin demanded.

Tears streamed down his face. He was shaking so hard that he could not be settled no matter how firmly Doyle held him. 'Say it! Say it!'

'I'll never leave you,' Doyle said, squeezing him even tighter. 'Oh, God, Colin, the two of you are all I have now. I've lost everything else now.'

The boy cried against his neck.

Carrying Colin, he went out of the kitchen and through the dining room, out to the main steps. 'We'll go and see how Courtney is,' he told the boy, hoping his voice would calm him.

It did not.

They were halfway up the steps towards the second floor when the boy began to shake worse than ever in Doyle's arms. 'Are you telling the truth? You really won't leave us?'

'Truth.' Doyle kissed the boy's tear-stained nose.

'Not ever?'

'Never. I told you . . . The two of you are all that's left. I've just lost everything else.'

Holding the boy against his chest as he went to see about Courtney, Alex thought that one of the things he had lost was the ability to cry as freely as a child. And right now, more than anything, he wanted to cry.

A selection of bestsellers from Headline

FICTION

THE DIETER	Susan Sussman	£3.99 ☐
TIES OF BLOOD	Gillian Slovo	£4.99 ☐
THE MILLIONAIRE	Philip Boast	£4.50 ☐
BACK TO THE FUTURE III	Craig Shaw Gardner	£2.99 ☐
DARKNESS COMES	Dean R Koontz	£3.99 ☐

NON-FICTION

THE WHITELAW MEMOIRS	William Whitelaw	£4.99 ☐
THE CHINESE SECRET SERVICE	Faligot & Kauffer Translated by Christine Donougher	£5.99 ☐

SCIENCE FICTION AND FANTASY

MAD MOON OF DREAMS	Brian Lumley	£3.50 ☐
BRIDE OF THE SLIME MONSTER Cineverse Cycle Book 2	Craig Shaw Gardner	£3.50 ☐
THE WILD SEA Bard III	Keith Taylor	£3.50 ☐

All Headline books are available at your local bookshop or newsagent, or can be ordered direct from the publisher. Just tick the titles you want and fill in the form below. Prices and availability subject to change without notice.

Headline Book Publishing PLC, Cash Sales Department, PO Box 11, Falmouth, Cornwall TR10 9EN, England.

Please enclose a cheque or postal order to the value of the cover price and allow the following for postage and packing:
UK: 80p for the first book and 20p for each additional book ordered up to a maximum charge of £2.00
BFPO: 80p for the first book and 20p for each additional book
OVERSEAS & EIRE: £1.50 for the first book, £1.00 for the second book and 30p for each subsequent book.

Name ....

Address ....

....

....